About the Author

Farzana Quader has had a long career in publishing, with a decade-long stint heading the English Language department of Oxford University Press, India. Her poems and short stories have been published in various prestigious journals, anthologies and literary magazines, like 'Selected Short Stories in Contemporary Indo-Anglian Literature', 'Indian Literature' published by Sahitya Academy of India, and 'The Times of India'. She received a special nomination in Muse India both for her prose and poetry. Her latest collection of poetry titled, '21 poems of Angst, Anxiety and Anguish' was published in 2021.

Shards of Glass

Farzana Quader

Shards of Glass

Olympia Publishers
London

www.olympiapublishers.com
OLYMPIA PAPERBACK EDITION

Copyright © Farzana Quader 2023

The right of Farzana Quader to be identified as author of
this work has been asserted in accordance with sections 77 and 78 of
the Copyright, Designs and Patents Act 1988.

All Rights Reserved

No reproduction, copy or transmission of this publication
may be made without written permission.
No paragraph of this publication may be reproduced,
copied or transmitted save with the written permission of the publisher,
or in accordance with the provisions
of the Copyright Act 1956 (as amended).

Any person who commits any unauthorised act in relation to
this publication may be liable to criminal
prosecution and civil claims for damage.

A CIP catalogue record for this title is
available from the British Library.

ISBN: 978-1-80074-899-6

This is a work of fiction.
Names, characters, places and incidents originate from the writer's
imagination. Any resemblance to actual persons, living or dead, is
purely coincidental.

First Published in 2023

Olympia Publishers
Tallis House
2 Tallis Street
London
EC4Y 0AB

Printed in Great Britain

Dedication

For Pitam, my first reader.

Jhuma 1

Butterflies flitted in the sky. The sun's rays came and nestled against her cheek, lighting up the green vein below her smooth transparent skin. It gleamed like a live snake. Jhuma's body quivered with each tug at the kite, a bright blob of red against the orange halo of the sun-tinted sky. Her eyes were specs of concentration, her body taut, poised in motion, balancing the movement of the kite in the sky. The wind caught the kite in a tight embrace and let it go with a playful jerk. With unlistening eyes, she strained against the wind to curb its gleeful play. For her it was no play. It was her fight to stretch her wayward soul beyond its limits—past all borders.

There was a tug from behind, an insistent tug. Then a soft voice rose to a shrill cry: 'Didi, didi, my yo-yo is broken. Mend it for me.'

Silently and slowly, she began to roll up the thread, drawing the skein closer to her, closer still, her eyes still intent on the red blob in the sky. As the glass-layered reddish thread wound itself around, the kite came to her grasp. She caught it smoothly in motion.

Then she bent down to the little creature, clamouring for her attention. Gruffly, she questioned, 'Yes, what's up? Why are you making such a noise?'

'Didi, my yo-yo. Mend it for me,' the six-year-old repeated his plea in a high plaintive tone.

'Come, I'll race you home. Here, hold my hand.'

They raced against the wind, their hands entwined in a tight clasp. The six-year-old's chubby fingers protected in the eighteen-year-old's firm grasp. As they came to a standstill at the porch of a whitewashed building, Jhuma took her breath. 'Bring me the yo-yo,' she instructed her brother in a serious tone. Bubai leapt to do her bidding.

Holding the spherical green object firmly in her left hand, Jhuma crouched on the porch. Bubai settled himself on her sloping shoulder, observing minutely. Jhuma turned the toy several times in a circular direction. Then, slipping her fingers through the groove, her fingers deftly undid the knots of the green cord. Holding both strands, she measured it in equal lengths and slipped it through the cleft again. Then, pulling the cord with one hand, she gingerly tested the yo-yo. It swayed in spring-like motions to the gentle tug of her hand. Satisfied with the little repair job, she handed the object to its rightful owner, who went off gleefully to play with it.

Jhuma could hear the chant of mantras floating in from the house. She pursed up her lips. 'Another niramish day. Now I have to put up with that terrible vegetable curry for lunch. Oh! How my mouth is watering for a tangy hilsa fish curry. Even the gods love to eat, don't they?'

At the doorway, Jhuma was greeted by a volley of barks from Bhola the Rampur greyhound, chained to a wall of the courtyard. She loosened him from his chain and fondled his ears. Madly happy at being released, Bhola rushed inside, barking to the dozen.

As Jhuma followed him, she was greeted by a chaotic scene. Bhola whizzed in like a dust-coloured tornado amidst the chants of the family priest. Ma, Didi and Boudi sitting reverently with their heads bowed in chaste devotion let out shrill cries beseeching Bhola to go away. *'Bhola, ja, ja.'* However, the attempts to restrain the dog were in vain. Bhola, heeding none, began to prance around the priest. At last, he had found the person responsible for his state of captivity before Jhuma's entry on the scene. The terrified priest, in a bid to escape this unexpected ordeal, hung precariously from the grandfather clock. The clock perched atop the polished teakwood almirah was a family heirloom inherited by Jhuma's grandfather, Satyajit Bandopadhyay, from her great-grandfather, the Late Honourable Nandalal Banerjei, along with five *bighas* of land as a token of appreciation for his services to the British. Jhuma, taking the scene at a glance, walked out of the room with laughter writ large on her face.

Tanya 1

As the short-statured 72-year-old Ibrahim Rahman walked into his granddaughter's room, his wrinkled face lit up with a smile. 'Did you enjoy the fish curry today, Tannu? Do I get an A plus for buying the right foodstuff from the bazaar?'

Tanya was sitting at her desk, poring over a historical novel. She instantly lowered the volume of the John Baez number playing on her stereo system.

'No, you have failed miserably. *C minus*. The fish had too many bones. I didn't even touch it. And pumpkin for vegetables, *yuck*. I hated it. Gee, *Dada*! You're a slow learner.'

The old man persisted: 'Failed with a C grade! Hahaha. So Tannu-ji, I'm a poor student. And what should be my penalty for this offence? Pay obeisance to Dadi-ji to make some lovely chana dal halwa for the evening snack? Or shall I fetch some piping hot s*amosas* to go with your tea?'

Tanya pulled out a chair for her grandfather. 'I don't want food. Our teacher has given us the booklist for the next class. When shall we buy these books, Dada?'

As Rahman Sahib settled himself into the chair, he took out his spectacles to look closely at Tanya's booklist. 'Shakespeare's *Merchant of Venice, Verity Edition, The Golden Treasury, Secondary Mathematics,* Julien Publishers... so, it's time for us to make our yearly pilgrimage to the Long John Stores, Tannu?'

'Yes,' said Tanya, as she good-humouredly removed her Dada's bifocal spectacles from his face and perched them on her nose. Then, taking out an old worn-out book from a shelf, she turned the yellowed pages and began to recite in a mock-humorous style:

'Let us go then, you and I
When the evening is spread out against the sky
Like a patient etherized upon a table
Let us go through certain half-deserted streets . . .'

'No, *hee, hee,* through the crowded streets of Calcutta to Long John Stores in Alinn's Road.'

'Oh, my, my, where did you pick that up? This must be that new-fangled Eliot who was your father's favourite poet. He composed such strange verses, comparing the beautiful evening sky to a patient under anaesthesia. Tch tch tch. . .'

'Not strange—these were the first lines of the *Love Song of Alfred J. Prufrock*. I discovered this old copy of Eliot's poetry in Abbu's bookshelf. It has Abbu's name and the year 1958 written on the flyleaf.'

'Fancy you reading this stuff at your age. You are hardly fourteen. Do you understand its meaning? Ah, your Abbu was a voracious reader too. But even he didn't start half as early as you. Real poetry is what we read in our times! Byron, Milton in English and Tagore in Bangla…'

Suddenly, the cosy tête-à-tête was interrupted by a bark from Hamletta as she came springing into Tanya's lap. 'Oh Hamletta, what's that in your mouth? Dada, look, she's got a laddu in her mouth.' Tanya broke into peals of laughter. 'Greedy girl, you must have stolen it from Dadi's larder.'

Rahman Sahib looked amused at the antics of his granddaughter's pet. He patted the dog on its head, who began to lick him all over. He had so far respected his wife's strictures not to allow an 'unclean creature' enter the house, spoiling the sanctity of her namaz. However, when his favourite granddaughter wanted one, even Dadi's objections could not deter him from bringing home a pet. Tanya had named the little white Spitz Hamletta. This was her coinage for a feminine version of Hamlet. Naughty and pert as the dog was, she always hesitated on the verge of her antics, confronted by the stern admonitions of Dadi. '*To do or not to do,*' Tanya would quote mockingly from her grandfather's repertoire of Shakespearean phrases.

Soon, Mama followed Hamletta into the room with a tray of halwa and pakoras and some dog biscuits for the pet. 'So, what are Dada and Granddaughter conspiring about?' she asked with a smile, as she laid the tray on Tanya's writing desk. 'No halwa for Hamletta, please,' she told the two, as she made an attempt to feed the dog his share of biscuits. 'I won't have him ill and throwing up all over the place if you feed him this ghee-rich stuff.'

'Oh Mum, how can you be so cruel? Look at him casting such greedy looks in our direction. We'll get a stomach upset for sure.' Sure enough, the dog was standing on its paws, drooling over the fragrant sweetmeat, rich with nuts, that Tanya's grandmother had prepared for them. Rina, Tanya's mother, laughed out aloud and fondly took Hamletta into her lap. 'Now, now, Hamu, come with me, I'll give you some bread and milk with sugar. Let Dada and Tannu eat in peace.'

'Bouma,' called out Rahman Sahib, motioning to his

daughter-in-law to wait. 'Tannu and I are planning to visit Long John Stores on Saturday to buy her books. Is there any story book that you require? You mentioned the other day that you wanted to read Ashapurna Devi's novel, *Subarnalata*. Should I get a copy for you?'

'Yes, Abba, I'll give you a list. And Amma wanted to listen to Rafi's qawwalis. Get a CD for her if it's available.'

'Okay, but I hope your mother-in-law will like the one I select.'

'Oh yes, she will.' Rina grinned at her father-in-law's remark as she left the room.

Angela 1

Mrs Jason drew the design herself and placed the order with the largest patisserie in town: Angela's birthday cake looked like a castle with little turrets, a moat and jutting balconies. Cake soldiers rode brown war horses in its fields. Nobles and ladies strolled in the parks and ladies-in-waiting perched on the benches in silent motion. The rose garden had a profusion of cake roses growing on it. The bakers covered the cake with transparent cellophane paper and ten coloured candles before delivering it.

Mrs Jason had started making preparations for the party a month ahead. It was her daughter's tenth birthday and it had to be the most talked about event of her town. Her sister-in-law sent her three metres of pink chiffon material from Singapore for which she travelled 300 kilometres from Jamshedpur to Calcutta. She chose an international design and the poshest tailor in Chowringhee.

Angela looked rather pretty in it, black curls accentuating the pink hue of her fair cheeks. Mrs Jason sighed when she thought of the day she was born. It was a shoddy hospital to give birth to her only child. The room looked like a kitchen and the nurses in their dirty uniforms—Ugh! She had been in such great pain, having a child at the late age of thirty-six. And all that the doctor and nurses could do was fool around with their tubes, while they gossiped among themselves. But that dark room lit up with the birth of her child. The doctor and nurses just gaped. They had seldom seen such a beautiful child. After her first glance at her granddaughter, her mama said: 'My, my! Your daughter looks as radiant as an angel.' So, they debated whether to call her Radiance or Angela.

The fool of her husband just stood around fiddling with her baby. As if he couldn't believe it was his own daughter. After all, his side of the family was pretty ugly. The beauty came from her side, no doubt about it. Mrs Jason recalled how people complimented her on her looks in her youth, with her long dark hair and grey eyes. Oh, she had so many admirers!

But she chose the wrong 'un and he made her life miserable. She had to cook and scrape because they couldn't afford to keep a maid for the first six years of her marriage. However, her daughter brought her luck. The tide turned when she met Ronnie, her ex-boyfriend at the hospital. He agreed to take her husband in his real estate business.

Soon, Jason learnt the ropes and struck out on his own—at her insistence—two years later... but he'd have been a good-for-nothing without her. She would have to bring up her daughter in penury. How life had changed! The Jasons were now the richest couple in town.

'Oh my, Mrs Pankaj and her family has already arrived. And the Robinsons are in tow, father and the two sons in dark corduroys, always so well-dressed. Thank God, Jason has gone up to receive them. Oh, look at that! Mrs Robinson is wearing a brilliant diamond necklace set in platinum. Looks more expensive than mine. Must be from Dubai. Hadn't she been there recently? She must tell Jason to get her one next time they go.'

'Hullo, Mrs Robinson! I'm so glad you could make it.'

'Oh no, Mrs Jason. We cut short our Switzerland trip just to attend your daughter's birthday.'

'Oh really! Tell me how was the Switzerland visit? Did you buy an original Omega? Last time Jason got me one.'

'Oh, no! Omega's dated. James got a Tissot for me and a Rado for himself. Do drop in some day, I'll show you my new collection of Swiss lace stoles. They're gorgeous. Here's some chocolates and cheese for you. Now, what a wonderful party you've organised. And where's darling Angela?'

'There she is! Angela dear, come and say "Hello" to Auntie Robinson.'

'Hello Auntie, how are you?'

'Oh, very well, dear. And look at you, how you've grown. Happy birthday, and here's a little gift for you. Marc chose it especially for you. I hope you like it.'

'Thank you, Auntie. I'm sure I will.'

By now the room had started filling up with Angela's parents' friends and their children. While Mrs Jason moved towards the other guests, the shy little girl hastened to make the acquaintance of the people whom her parents introduced her to. The waiters in their starched white uniforms served the guests refreshments and drinks and the hall echoed with the laughter and chatter of the visitors. A pianist in a corner entertained the guests with a light water music followed by some études of Chopin.

After Angela cut the cake to much cheering, couples took to the dance floor in tune with swinging rhythms put up by a well-known veejay. This was followed by a belly-dance by the famous Lolita.

Angela wandered around the room for some time with a fixed smile on her lips. Then she slipped quietly into the garden when she observed her parents occupied with the niceties of the evening. Her head ached and she was dying for a breath of cool air. She went to her favourite hideout, and sat on the old swing rocking herself to and fro. 'How I wish Mum didn't call these boring people to celebrate my birthday. I wish Meena and Tim could come instead and we could have a party—just the three of us. But Mum doesn't like them and she wouldn't call them over because they are not rich. She says they have bad manners and the clothes they wear are positively shocking. How does it matter what they wear? I like them and it's supposed to be my party. I'm so lonely. I have nobody to play with. I know what I'll do. I'll ask Dad for his mobile and call up Meena.'

Thrilled with the thought, Angela ran into the crowded room again and went straight up to her father. 'Dad, I want your mobile. I have to talk to a friend.' Mr Jason handed her the mobile and told her, 'Take it, dear, but do bring it back quickly. I'm expecting an important call from Germany.'

'Yes, Dad,' replied Angela as she hurriedly ran back to her swing. Fiddling with the mobile, she called up Meena whose landline number she knew by heart.

'Meena, it's me Angela. Were you sleeping?'

'Hullo Angela. Happy birthday… for the second time today. How was the cake?' Angela heard Meena's chirpy laughter and instantly her spirits revived.

'Guess what! The cake was beautiful. It looked exactly like a castle I saw in an old English movie. Mum copied the design and they made it with cake. And there were lovely flowers in the garden. I'll bring lots for tiffin tomorrow. You can all have it. I'll show you the snapshots too. What are you doing now?'

'I'm playing with my brother Arun. He's just learning to toddle and it's so funny watching him. He stumbles and falls every few steps. I'm teaching him how to walk properly.'

'Oh, what fun, I wish I had a little brother or sister to play with. It's so boring here. The hall's full of funny people wearing such strange dresses and smelling of sick perfume. Ugh!'

'Poor dear Angela. You sleep tight today, tomorrow we'll play a new game in school.'

'Okay. I have to give this phone back to Dad. Otherwise, he'll come looking for me. Bye, Meena, sweet dreams.'

'Bye.'

Then Angela went back to the hallway and told her mother that she was sleepy.

'Okay, run off, dear. But before you leave, wish Aunt Matilda, Aunt Advani and all your cousins good-night. Don't forget to tell Marc—he brought a special gift for you all the way from Switzerland, remember?'

'Yes Mum.'

After obediently wishing everyone a good night, Angela ran upstairs where Ayah was waiting to put her into her night clothes.

Angela chatted with Ayah about the events of the evening. Then she snuggled into bed with Evelina, her rag doll. Her parents had brought her the most expensive dolls from the countries they visited. And her mother tried hard to persuade her to discard the broken rag doll. It was a reminder of the times when they could only afford to buy such cheap toys for their precious daughter. But Angela wouldn't let it go. She wept piteously every time her mother tried to take the doll away. Now she clutched it tightly and as Ayah put off the lights, Angela whispered, 'Sleep, Mamma, sleep', cuddling up to her doll cosily.

Jhuma 2

Jhuma's eyes were fixed on the goal, her eyes alert to every movement on the field, her body alive to the ongoing action; an action that would bring her the required victory. Yes, Jhuma would have to score the last goal to save her team. She was captain of "East Side Team A". The match had begun on an exciting note. Jhuma's team had scored the first goal against "West Zone Kanchrapara". Her friends cheered her hoarse. Then for a long time the two teams played tooth and nail. West Zone put up a splendid defence. But soon after the whistle blew for the second half, the latter scored a goal. They equalled the score. Now it was 1-1.

It put Jhuma in a frenzy. She must win this game at all costs. Her favourite player Riltoo played two wonderful shots. But their goalkeeper was quicker. Three minutes left. The last goal for East Side was yet to be scored. The minutes ticked by slowly, and just before the end, West Zone did the trick. The ball sped past Shyam straight into the goal. Oni, the East Side goalkeeper was left gaping. Jhuma threw down her cap and shook hands with the West Zone captain Debabrata.

There was loud booing and catcalls from their side of the stand. They were jeering at her: 'Go, girl, sit at home and wait for your husband! Go, girl, sit at home, cook fish and dal for him.' Anger welled up in her. Her face red with humiliation, she stalked away from the field. How dare they? It was an even game and her team had put up a spirited fight. What did their defeat have to do with her being a girl? She played as well as any of them. Last year when East Side lost 2-0 under the captaincy of Shubho, these same fellows had come to console him. '*Go, sit at home yourselves, you nincompoops*,' muttered Jhuma under her breath.

***

Feeling restless, she started walking past the known lanes and bylanes till she reached the crossing of Rupganj. Then she walked straight towards the marsh. Most elders warned them against traversing this lonely stretch alone. They believed anything could happen in this dangerous stretch, from robbery to rape. But today Jhuma was in no mood to brook a care.

The putrid and damp smell of the marsh reached Jhuma's nose from a distance. After reaching the spot, she sat on a broken culvert overlooking the wasteland. The air was cool and restful. There were hordes of butterflies swarming about. She had never seen so many at a time. As she stared gloomily into space in the failing light, she could hear the members of the Bal Seva Samiti engrossed in their workouts across the marsh. *One Two, One Two, One. Left Right, Left Right, Left*. The cheerless sound of the leader's instructions floated to her ears. As she stared in contempt at the shadowy figures far away, Jhuma grinned to herself: 'Pooh! These pious hulks with filthy minds. They took the oath of Brahmacharya, didn't they?' Then a thought struck her, filling her with hilarity: if she had a chance to be their leader for a few days, she'd turn them into proper daredevils. What fun it would be to reverse the order. *Swear words: yes.*

Hard rock: yes. Rap dance: yes. Love: yes. Lust: no... Picking pockets: no. A clean people, a clean country: yes, yes, yes.

Jhuma sighed and was about to leave when she discovered that the ritualistic drills were over. The members were departing one by one. Suddenly in the darkness she heard voices close by. Kishore, whom she knew well, was in deep conversation with a lean and tall boy. They came and sat on the ledge opposite the bridge. Kishore was talking while his companion listened intently... *something about the factory workers at Rohra. The owners had started a riot. They had a hand in the murder of a worker. The riot led to a slash of pay rates.* Jhuma listened. So, Kishore posed to be a member of the Bal Seva. He was not really one of them. Suddenly it struck her like a bolt. He was doing what Jhuma had thought of playfully. Subverting the order of the Samiti by educating their members secretly. Up down up. Jhuma's being awoke to a sense of thrill.

Tanya 2

Tanya stared out of the open window. Fields, ponds, cows, huts, bare-bodied men and naked children went by in a rush. Women bent low over flooded rice-fields with their saris riding high over their knees. The train gathered speed. Her body seemed to be in perfect synchrony with its rolling movement. Journeys always made her slightly heady with their sense of the unknown. She wondered what it would be like to get off at one of those stations where the express train hardly seemed to pause at. There was an urge to walk off into these unexplored paths and learn about the people there. To partake of the myriad strangeness of those lives lived out in oblivion!

Thoughts flitted in and out of Tanya's head. Yesterday there was a letter from the Tribal Centre in Auckland University. They had offered to fund her PhD on the Maoris. She had always been fascinated by the Maori tribes. As a child, she had read how they had sailed forth from their mythical homeland 'Hawaiki' in the Polynesian islands and sailed forth in large ocean-going 'wakas'. Then they arrived in an uninhabited land full of bird-life. They hunted the moa bird in large numbers and came to be known as the 'moa-hunters'. It might be a good idea to steer her research work in the direction of a contrasting study with the Toda and Kota tribes of the Nilgiris. Her application to Maryland University in the USA had also got a positive response. But she was hesitant about going to the States. She'd have access to the best libraries and documented research available there, no doubt. But wouldn't it be like working in a sterile laboratory with little scope for interaction with live tribal culture? Besides, could she afford to make so many flying trips to New Zealand for her field work on the Maoris?

Suddenly, Tanya's reverie was interrupted by a three-year-old child's voice asking 'Didi' if she could sit by the window and look out. Tanya smiled at the child and said, 'I will let you sit near the window, but first you have to answer my questions.' The child shyly looked up at her father who nodded to show encouragement. 'Tell Didi your name, then she will let you sit by the window.'

Tanya took the child on her lap. 'Didi knows your name. It's Ananya, isn't it? Now look at that—what's that over there?' 'Dog,' said the child in a small voice. Tanya chatted with the child until she fell asleep, lulled by the rolling movement of the train. She gently picked up the sleeping child and laid her on the empty berth beside her. The train stopped at Vijaywada, which was an important junction. She could hear the vendor's cry announcing idlis and baras. She went up to the door to buy some food and tea for her dinner.

As the train left the station, her thoughts flew homewards. I wonder what Ammu and Dadi are doing now? They would be watching their favourite serial, speculating all the while who would marry whom. She sorely missed Dada. The incident came back to her clearly. She was just into the second semester of her post-graduation in the *Gandhi School of Social Anthropology* in Delhi. That year she'd bagged the coveted teaching assignment which would see her through the fourth semester, having topped her class. Congratulations poured in. And all the while Ammu and Dadi kept harping about a marriage proposal for her which they found too tempting to let go.

The first shock came with the arrival of Ammu's email: *twenty-nine years old... good family... met his mother and sister on their way back to Mumbai from Singapore... he is heading the Singapore Division of the US Syndicate Bank as Vice President... Dadi and I have arranged for you to meet him when you come home for your summer leave.*

Would her family support her decision to go to New Zealand? How persuasive they were. But that meeting with the pompous fool of a Mr Collins incarnate hardened her resolve: an Americanised accent, a flashy car, his views on democracy and freedom in the US, and he had the gall to say that Indian women were behind times.

Her hackles rose. 'What about Chomsky,' she chipped in. 'Why is he backstaged by the Western media? Why doesn't the "Free Press" hardly ever highlight his views? Because he is openly critical of their policies? What about the agenda-ridden foreign and military policies of intervention? Why do Western women feel insecure if they don't have a "date"? And tell me why, Sir, does the whole of their cosmetic industry pander to make their women look young? Are these signs of their progressiveness?'

Mr Vice President clearly didn't care for such outspokenness in Indian women. When they left, there was a stillness about the house. Dadi's face reflected the huff while Ammu's face hid it. Ma mumbled something about having brought her up to respect guests. What about the fact that that guy did not respect either his own country nor its women?

And yet he wanted to marry a desi girl...

Would it have been different if Dada had been alive? He

had always encouraged her to be independent.

Her mind went back to a day way back in the past. Grandy and she had gone to purchase books for the first booklist of her school year from Long John Stores in Alinn's Road. She was five years old. Holding Dada's hand, they walked to the tram stop. It was a hot summer afternoon. Several crowded trams came by, but Grandy said they would wait for an empty one. The 25-number to Howrah was empty and the conductor waited to ring the bell for the tram to start after they got up. Tanya found an empty seat beside the window and Grandy sat beside her. She loved the rolling movement of the tram ride. The seat was marked 'For Senior Citizens only'. She did not know what it meant. Dada explained to her that it was reserved for old people like him, that is anybody who had crossed sixty years of age. She remembered she had told him that in that case she should not be sitting there. Dada was delighted to discover that his young grandchild had such a keen sense of justice. He told her, 'Yes, dear, that is true. So, if an old person comes by, young lady, you have to give up your place to him or her.'

On the way they passed Eliot Road. Many people boarded the tram and soon it was full of people standing. They passed one school and she saw lots of little children come out. School was a big wonder then as she was just waiting to start school. A mother holding a three-year-old child in her lap and a seven-year-old by the hand was standing in front of their seat. Dada got up and asked the lady politely to sit in his seat. An old man standing nearby protested, 'Sir, if you are giving up your seat, by rights I should sit there.' 'Sure, Sir, you are right. And my granddaughter will gladly vacate her seat for you. But let the lady sit, she's finding it difficult to stand with her two daughters and their heavy school bags.' Her little heart had swelled with pride for her grandfather. When their Wellington stop came, she got down holding Grandy's hand—'Grandy', that was the name she had given him!

As Dada and her five-year-old self got off the tram, they were greeted by the signboard of a large departmental store called Long John. She could still feel the wonder of discovering the old shop with Dada. It was cool and dark inside. Toy cycles and dolls were displayed in the shop window. Salesmen were showing some people navy blue school sweaters at a counter. Children's red and yellow umbrellas were stacked in one corner. She loved the smell and the colours. They went to the book counter where Grandy showed them her booklist where he had marked certain things with a blue pencil. The man brought out her Big Book of ABC and laid it on the counter. It smelled new and the picture of the red apple on the blue cover stared back at her. That was her very first book. The journey that was to bring her here. She and Grandy had come out proudly holding a big brown paper packet. In it were all the things Tanya would need for school. That was how she was prepared to begin school in Convent of Mother Mary.

Later, the visit to Long John with Dada became a yearly pilgrimage that lasted till his death.

The train had stopped midway between stations again. Ananya had woken up from her nap. After they completed their dinner, a slightly older child from the next berth joined her and they were both merrily reciting all the nursery rhymes. Tanya remembered how pleased Grandy would be when she recited the poems that she learnt in school. But she could not draw very well. Once for their drawing test in Kindergarten, her friend Peter drew a yellow duck swimming about in a splash of blue water. When they got their report cards, he'd got an 'A' and she got a 'C' in Drawing.

'Never mind,' Grandy would say, 'you've got A's in all the other subjects. And Tannu, dear, you can read your brother Sani's Graham Reader like a duck taking to water.' She was so obsessed with the written word that she would read whatever books she could lay her hands on. When Sani, who was two years older than her, came for his summer vacation from his boarding school in Ranchi, she would read all the stories in his English textbooks. The Graham Readers had such lovely pictures and stories, recalled Tanya. On one double spread page there was a picture of an overturned glass of milk. One of the child characters, Pat or Tom, had dropped it. The words said, *'There's no use crying over spilt milk.'* What an ingenious way of combining the figurative meaning with the literal. She had never forgotten those words: 'There's no use crying over spilt milk.'

Once, she had fever and Amma would not let her go to school. She was so angry with her mother for making her miss school. There was a Maths test. On that occasion she was quite sore because even Grandy sided with her mother. He said, 'You've got good grades, and besides, you can make up in the next term. As a mark of protest, she refused to have her meals the entire day. Amma and Grandy coaxed her and cajoled her but she would not as much touch the soup. Finally, they relented and allowed her to go to school the next day.

Dadi's favourite quote was 'When Tanya grows up, she'll be like Indira Gandhi', a woman who, in her grandmother's view, epitomised the height of success. She was then eight years old and had scribbled in her diary one night, *'Can Indira Gandhi fly? I want to fly; to spread my wings and fly ever so high, into the sky.'*

How strange it is, thought Tanya. Dadi, you wanted me to lead the nation once. Where have all those dreams gone? I wonder whether Grandy would have understood my aspirations! Or would he too want me to follow the beaten track?

Tanya's rebelliousness came to the fore. Staring out, her soul thirsted for a touch with the soil. She knew this was no passing fancy. It represented the vital core of her existence. Would her soul's desire ever be played out in the canvas of her life?

Angela 2

Angela and Marc's wedding had been fixed for December the seventh. Hectic preparations were on, but everything seemed to go wrong at the last minute. Angela's wedding gown was late in arriving from Mumbai. When it did arrive, it was loose at the waist. So, last minute alterations had to be made by the local tailor. A cyclone that caused havoc in the city two days before the wedding caused extensive damage to the powerlines of the church. Workmen were put on the job round-the-clock and power was restored on the morning of the wedding. Angela wished to carry a bouquet of white roses to match with the finely embroidered tiny white roses in her wedding gown. But on the day of the wedding there were none to be found. She had to be contented with a bunch of yellow ones.

When the bride finally walked up the aisle of St Thomas' Cathedral, she was nothing but a bundle of nerves. But all went well and they exchanged vows and rings without further mishaps. At the end of the ceremony, when Marc's lips brushed hers with the priest declaring them 'man and wife', Angela felt her happiness was complete. For the evening reception, she wore a green silk sari matched with an emerald set glittering on her neck and ears. Standing beside the handsome Marc Robinson, the two made a pretty picture. They smiled and chatted with the steady stream of visitors who came up to congratulate them.

Angela recalled how Mama and Papa had been only too happy to announce her betrothal to Marc Robinson, junior partner of Glowdell Finances and son of industrialist Andrew Robinson. The two families were delighted at the union of their children.

As Angela surreptitiously stole a look of adoration at Marc, she thought of the first time that she had met him in her childhood. 'Angela, dear,' Mama had called out. She had come skipping into their sitting room in Lansdowne Square. Her mother introduced her to the Robinsons, their new neighbours who had just moved into the big bungalow next door. Mama had asked her to recite a poem and from her stock of nursery rhymes she rattled off, '*Mary, Mary, quite contrary.*' Everyone in the room clapped, except the twelve-year-old Marc who teased her.

'Angela, are you contrary like Mary?'

Mamma, who was immensely sensitive about her daughter, swiftly answered back, 'No, my Angela is a darling. If I forbid her to do something, she always listens to me. What's more, unlike other children, she never forgets to say Grace before her meals, don't you darling? Now go and do your homework, dear.'

Angela went in obediently. Within a year, however, the Robinsons had moved to Mumbai, and that was the end of their association. It was merely six months back that she had been invited along with her parents to a party thrown by her father's classmate. Uncle James had returned to India recently, after his retirement from the United Nations in Geneva. Angela had just turned eighteen and was enrolled in college. For the party she had worn black trousers with a green silk shirt, and cosmetic jewellery and fashionable high heels to complete the outfit. Her thick black hair as usual framed her oval face in curls. Marc later said that she looked striking in green—that is why she had chosen to wear green for her reception today.

At the party, Uncle James had reintroduced them. Marc had asked her for the first dance. After that, they'd spent the whole evening virtually together. Between dances, they sat down to chat and share drinks. The whole evening seemed like a fairy tale experience, a dream that she had been waiting to realise since she was a child. When at the end of it, Marc asked her for a date the following Saturday, she could hardly refuse him. But she said she would ask Mama for permission, and he politely replied that he would wait for her call.

Mama and Papa were happy to know that they had got along well, and soon they started dating each other with feverish impatience. Within a short time, Marc proposed. She felt elated and so were her parents. The families planned a grand wedding. The *who's who* of Bombay and Delhi had flown down to attend it. She would have preferred a simple affair with close friends and family. But Marc wanted it to be a magnificent affair…

Suddenly, Angela's thoughts were diverted by a spectacle at the entrance of the hall. She could hear faint voices in the background—someone pleading to be let in! The gateman was blocking the person's entry. The next instant, she heard her mother's stern voice instructing the guard, '*Durwanji*, ask her to leave immediately. This is not the place for the likes of her. It's full of VIPs. Security is a major concern. We cannot allow rifraffs like her.'

As realization dawned on Angela, she ran to the spot. 'Ayah! Ayah! I'm so glad that you're here. Don't go away. Let her in, please.'

With these words, she led the old haggard woman by the hand to the centre of the hall. 'Marc, this is Ayah. Remember I spoke to you about my childhood days when Ayah used to pamper me and tell me stories. I'm so happy that she's here to bless me on my wedding day.' With this, she turned to the other guests and said, 'I'm so proud to introduce you all to Ayah, who took care of me as a child and means so much to me. I'm overjoyed that she's here on the most important day of my life.'

The old woman said, 'Bless you, child. When I heard that it was your wedding day, I came to give you this cotton doll that I stitched myself. Remember how you loved playing with your broken rag doll as a child. You're grown up now, but keep this as a token of remembrance from me. God bless you, dear. Now, I'll take leave of you all.' Wiping her eyes, Ayah quietly left the room, stooping slightly with the burden of her age. Angela fondly clasped the rag doll, still warm with Ayah's touch.

Jhuma 3

Jhuma thought hard about Kishore's involvement with the Bal Seva. Why had he joined the Samiti? What was his real purpose? She must meet him and unearth his plan. She had heard that he lived somewhere in Rupganj.

On Monday morning, Jhuma started early for college. On the way, she went first to Kishore's house. He was getting ready to leave and was surprised to see her.

'Anything wrong?' He was concerned, looking at Jhuma's pale face.

'Kishore-da, I want to talk to you.'

'What about? Have those Kanchrapara boys been troubling you again?'

'No, it's not that. I can't talk to you here. Will you come with me to the marsh?'

'The marsh?' Kishore hesitated momentarily. 'Okay, let's go. But won't you be late for college?'

'It doesn't matter.' Jhuma brushed off the subject.

Kishore headed for the marsh on his bike, with Jhuma riding pillion. Just before reaching the bridge, he brought the vehicle to a standstill.

'Tell me, what has disturbed you.'

'I was sitting here the other day and I heard your conversation.'

'Which day and what conversation?' asked Kishore blankly.

'Oh, it was Friday and I was feeling restless. I came here for a walk. The Bal Seva workouts were just getting over. Then you came and sat here talking to a tall fair boy about the factory workers of Rohra. Kishore-da, you don't really belong to the Bal Seva, do you? I don't like them and I think you don't, either?'

Kishore looked at Jhuma silently for a while.

Then he spoke slowly, softly: 'What do you think? What is my real purpose in being there?'

'I think you belong to the Working People's Movement and you're fighting for their rights. Is it true, Kishore-da?'

'Yes, you've come close to the truth. I'm part of the WGM, the Worker's Grassroot Movement. Our real work lies with the poor factory workers and peasants toiling in oppressed conditions, even seventy years after our liberation from the British. Our politicians and capitalist-owners have joined hands to make mincemeat of them. And the reason for my association with the Bal Seva Samiti is simply our concern for the fresh young youth lured by these jingoistic outfits. So, we select some of the bright young fellows hoping to alter their political perspective. Our concern is to prevent them all from going the reactionary way. The boy I was talking to the other day is Jeet, a fresh and intelligent recruit, who hasn't yet been ingrained into their orthodox thinking.'

Jhuma listened wide-eyed. As Kishore paused for breath, she spoke out boldly: 'Kishore-da, I want to join the WGM as an active member.'

Kishore studied Jhuma's face and then he said softly:

'Do you know the risks involved?'

'I have never cared for risks.'

Kishore thought about it for a while and said, 'Okay Jhuma, we'll talk about it again. There are many things you need to know before you plunge in. I'll take you to our District Head next week. Let me drop you at college meanwhile.'

Jhuma nodded silently. Oh, how could she explain to him with what passion she would devote herself to the cause, if only he showed her the way.

***

Mrs Bithi Sen, the President of the Zilla committee, clad in a white sari with a brown border, looked at Jhuma askance: 'Upside down! And what may I infer from your statement, Miss Sanyal, that you want to turn things upside down? The system, presumably?'

Jhuma, undeterred said, 'Yes, that and the Bal Seva Samiti.'

'Please do understand that we are not here to merely dislodge the Bal Seva. The Bal Seva is of course a minute expression of a dangerous intent. It is the intention that we have to fight with. We have a higher purport in view, that is to reverse the status quo, the social order, to give our grassroot workers their due share in the fruits of labour. Is it clear, Miss Sanyal? I shall give you some of our printed discourses which you must go through very carefully.'

'Yes, Ma'am,' said Jhuma, in a muted voice.

'Bithi, dear, you are scaring her out of her wits, and we may be on the verge of losing a fine worker on the very first day,' interrupted a moustachioed jeans-clad figure as he walked into the room, with a *biri* perched between his fingers.

'Jhuma, this is Raghunath-da, our Zilla Chief Secretary.' Kishore introduced the tall smiling man.

'Yes, Jhuma, you were saying something about turning things upside down. I think you've hit the kernel with one dart. Reversing the order would be expressed in your young language, I suppose, as "upside down". And the rest you will pick up by and by. Meanwhile, this is for you.' Raghunath took out a sheaf from his yellow cloth bag and gave it to her.

'What is it, Raghunath-da?' asked Jhuma eagerly, her recently dampened spirits brightening up instantly.

'It is a collection of folk songs sung by the farmers in Egypt during their harvest season. There is a lot of similarity in tune and lyrics with the harvest songs sung in our own countryside. Do you like music?'

'Oh yes, I do.'

'Okay, you take this along with the treatises that Bithi is giving you. Those tomes will stimulate your intellect while the music will stir your heart.'

'Raghunath-da, what will be my first assignment?' asked Jhuma eagerly.

'Your first assignment! Ha! Ha! Ha!' laughed Raghunath out loud. 'Very eager to take off, eh? Well, Bithi, Kishore, what assignment should we give Jhuma—something terrible to frighten her off?'

Bithi Sanyal said, 'Since you've put music before our party ideology, you better decide what should be Miss Sen's first assignment!'

'Oh, Bithi dear, she's just a youngster, call her Jhuma. And you'll see music will take her faster into our party ideology than those dusty tomes of yours can. Perhaps the first job she can do is to organise a musical event for the WGM workers. How would that do for you, Jhuma?'

Jhuma was a little taken aback. While she had visions of leading a farmers' rally and delivering herself to a lathi-charging police force, or at least giving a fiery speech at a workers' meeting, here was Raghunath-da asking her to organise a musical event as if it were an ordinary college event!

Jhuma nodded silently in assent.

Tanya 3

Tanya looked at her working notes in the dimly lit compartment of the North Indian Express. Six hours to go and she would be arriving at Coimbatore. From there, a five-hour drive would take her to the Nilgiris. Murugan would be there to meet her at Coonoor and after breakfast they would head off for a tribal village 150 km into the interior. She mused on Murugan, her erstwhile college classmate. Although he'd scored brilliantly in his BA finals, he opted out of postgraduate studies unlike the rest of the class. Tanya had tried hard to persuade him to continue his studies. Murugan decided to settle down among the Kota tribe who lived in near complete isolation. He was one of the rare outsiders whom they accepted as one of their own.

***

The old tribal woman smiled at Tanya. She touched her hand and indicated towards Murugan. 'My child,' she said in her language. '*Soim* (God) has sent him as a gift for me. He calls me *Perav* (Grandmother).'

Tanya looked in the direction she pointed. Murugan was helping the Kota children knit some palm fronds into braids for rope. Scattered around him were the charcoal sketches he had done of the children. Tanya felt excluded from the quiet deep bonding that he shared with the Kotas. It was only as Murugan's friend that Tanya had got the rare privilege of associating with this exclusive fraternity.

Tanya was staying in the only pukka house within a range of ten kilometres. It was an abandoned government building built in the previous regime to serve as an office for gathering census data about the Nilgiri tribes. The dismal state of the building proclaimed the feeble intention of the administration and its failure at one go. Murugan had fitted up one of its rooms with some bare furnishings for her to stay.

'Muru,' began Tanya, as they walked back towards her lodgings, 'you know about the research project that I have decided to take up in Auckland. I'll have to make many field trips to this part. I think they will really help to deepen my insight into the tribal culture of the Nilgiris.'

'You think so?'

'You don't? What about your own plans? Will you continue working with the Kotas or move over to the Todas? By the way, I don't see you gathering data for your work? Aren't you submitting your research on the Kotas for an UGC grant?'

'No, I'm not doing this for any project.'

'What do you mean, Muru? I know working with a supervisor for a PhD would constrain you but you could easily submit a wonderful thesis for a doctorate with the close-up view of the tribals that you already possess. You have adequate data to back you up—the only obstacle in your way of not possessing an MA degree can be overcome easily. Appear for the exam through correspondence mode. Scoring a First Class is going to be a cakewalk for you…'

'What would I do with a PhD? How would it help me or them?'

'Oh Muru, I don't have to explain that to you. Now tell me

what's your plan for the future? To become an anthropologist or an artist?'

'Perhaps a bit of both and neither of either,' chuckled Murugan. 'But why do you want to go to Auckland and waste your time there? Do you think those tomes in the library or all the professors who make occasional field trips can really enlighten you about tribal life? What will all those years you spend in those synthetic labs really fetch you? A doctoral degree, a professorship, some research papers! Wouldn't it be far more meaningful if you stayed on with these people here?'

'Stay on doing what?'

'Living and understanding tribal life—the beginnings of social existence.'

'No, Muru, I can't do that. I can't give up Auckland and my PhD and stay on here aimlessly.'

'Not aimlessly. But with a new aim and a new beginning.'

'I don't understand what you're saying.'

'Try, Tanya, you can if you want to. They are dying of disease and starvation because we have uprooted them from their natural state. Their way of life is endangered. We have to save them.'

'Yes, that is exactly what I want to do. But to do so, I need to be better equipped with my research on them.'

'They need you more than Auckland does.'

They had reached the crossroads which led to Tanya's lodgings. Murugan usually said goodbye to her at this juncture.

'Tomorrow, I'll take you to the *Kamatra-ya* festival held for praying to the rain gods and their titular deity... Meet me here,' called out Murugan as he turned towards the Kovvillage. The rays of the setting sun fell on his retreating figure, lighting up his profile with a strange glow.

'Bye,' said Tanya, moving forward to enter the decrepit building.

Angela 3

Angela looked up from beneath her long eyelashes at the profile of her husband. He was having a nap on the aircraft seat beside her. They were returning from their honeymoon trip after a brief stopover at Mumbai. Events of the past month crowded in her memory.

Her wedding had been celebrated in high style, with celebrities flown down from all quarters. The wedding was followed by a long week filled with dinner invitations and parties thrown in their honour.. After that, she and Marc had spent their honeymoon cruising in the Caribbean and lounging in beaches. On their way back, Marc wished to spend a week in Mumbai, golfing and clubbing with his friends. Gosh! If only they didn't bump into Uncle Suresh and Aunt Ruby. They were Dad's first cousins, but Mama had not invited them for her wedding. She said that they would stick out like a sore thumb among all the glitterati. And Dad said the couple would not be able to afford the plane fare—so why bother? But they were as affectionate as ever when they met Marc and her. They just would not listen to the young couple's pleas to wriggle out of the invitation. Their house was in a dirty lane in Chorpatty. Marc didn't even touch the food that Aunt Ruby took such efforts to prepare. Angela had to make a dozen excuses like Marc had a headache and so on. And to top it! Once they were back in the privacy of their hotel room, Marc was absolutely furious with her for harbouring such 'gross relatives'.

Although she'd spent a lot of intimate time with Marc, she did not feel as if she knew him as well as she did earlier. *It was if his mask had slipped...* Oh no! How did those words slip out? Something about Marc's attitude towards her parents too had changed after their wedding. He had got along splendidly with them earlier. But when Dad called up a couple of hours after they set sail, he sounded dour and surly. Did he resent the intrusion? He replied to her father only in monosyllables... Strange, he was quite chatty when his own parents called up later that night... Anyway, she would soon get busy with doing up her new house in Bangalore. It was a palatial one and there would be umpteen things to do. I wonder if we'll be entertaining a lot.

Six months later...

Angela looked at the dining room clock for the hundredth time perhaps in the past quarter of the hour. When would Marc be back? She could hardly wait to show him the cradle, the pram and the toys she had bought that morning. He was really getting busier than ever with his whirlwind tours and business meetings. But he would soon have to cut down on them, Angela smiled to herself. As Mama says, fathers always make time for their little ones, no matter what!

A pang of doubt struck Angela. Would he like the baby things that she had bought from *Kids' Store*?

He always liked the best, he said. And he had made such a fuss the last time she had bought a whole lot of household furnishings. He'd said they looked cheap and tawdry compared to the designer stuff his interior decorator got from abroad. But somehow Angela did not care for the cold and fancy things that Miss Kirsten had put up everywhere. She wanted the house to look cosy and warm.

Anyway, the baby was coming and as her Mum and aunts advised her, she must be very cheerful. She could feel it moving in her stomach. Maybe the baby would bring Marc and her closer, and they'd have some quiet evenings to themselves. She was tired of the parties—the crowds, the glitter, the dance, the drinks and the diamonds!

Jhuma 4

Jhuma stooped to enter one of the low, narrow doorways of the Jangipara slum. The sun was beating mercilessly outside. Wiping the sweat off her forehead, she called out, 'Sipra-di, how is Lotika?'

Sipra got up from the mat. 'Oh Didi, you've come. The entire night she had high fever. She was groaning and tossing while I kept applying wet patches on her forehead to keep her cool. Finally, she fell asleep around dawn. Hasn't sipped a drop of water since then.'

Jhuma took out the medicines from her bag. 'I've spoken to Dr Sengupta. He's prescribed these capsules and a syrup. The capsules have to be taken every six hours and the syrup twice a day after meals.'

Sipra said, 'Should I give them to her now?'

Jhuma replied, 'No, wait a minute, she must have something to eat first. I've got these ingredients for a light soup. Prepare a bowl of soup first. Then, she can have the medicine. Once the fever subsides, you can give her the fruits.'

Sipra nodded and put the things away. Jhuma felt Lotika's forehead. It was burning hot. She took out a thermometer and noted the temperature in a notebook. Then she sponged the child's face and hands with a wet towel while Sipra prepared fresh soup. After feeding Lotika, her mother cleaned and dusted the bed.

As Jhuma got up to go, she said, 'I almost forgot, here is

the leaflet for the WGM meeting next Tuesday.'

Sipra said, 'Don't go, Jhuma-didi. Let me brew some tea for both of us. I've also not put a morsel in my mouth since last night.'

As they sipped the tea with puffed rice, Sipra said, 'Jhuma-didi, you're so educated and well-read, perhaps you can tell me of what use are these meetings? They say so many things about rights and justice, but how does it touch our lives? We're in the same condition as before, nothing changes for us. So many times, I've told them to open a school for our girls in Jangipara so that they don't have to travel all the way to Daulatpur, but who listens? And the doctor *babus* hardly ever comes to the medical centre in our area. And if we go to his assistant Sunil for medicines, he asks for money. There's hardly enough for food, where do we have the money to buy tablets? If it hadn't been for you, I don't know how I could have taken care of Lotika's treatment.'

Jhuma listened to her in silence. Then she told Sipra, 'I'll have to go now, I have other work to do. Meanwhile, don't forget to give Lotika the capsules. I'll come again tomorrow.'

Jhuma turned left towards the main road and walked on till she reached Jalil Khan's house. His grandchildren, Salma, Sumi, Khalil and Jahanara were playing outside. They came running up to her. 'Jhuma-didi, Jhuma-didi, Sumi and I have finished reading the storybook you gave us last time,' said Jahanara.

'I liked the story of the *Magic Sword* the best,' said Sumi. 'I want to be a magician when I grow up.'

'Oh, do you? That's a wonderful ambition,' said Jhuma. 'But remember Sumi, a magician has to work very hard, speak very well, and be a wonderful performer to earn his living. Have you heard of PC Sorkar, the great magician? I'll take you to one of his shows.'

'I also want to go,' said Salma and Khalil together.

'Don't take Khalil. He never does his lessons properly. Grandfather scolded him yesterday,' complained Jahanara.

'Khalil, you must finish those five lessons I marked for you. Then I'll take you all for the show. Now I must go and meet your Nana.'

Jalil Khan, a tall spare austere figure, with a head of grey hair, clad in white kurta-pyjamas, was sitting on an armchair in the veranda, writing an article.

'Jalil-da, how are you?' Jhuma took out the leaflet and gave it to him. He read it carefully and nodded his head. 'Okay, I'll be there.'

Then he paused a minute and said, 'Well, Jhuma, do you know why Sumanto and Tapan haven't come to discuss with me anything about writing the editorial piece for *Jago Samaj* this time? It should have gone to the Press by now.'

Jhuma remained silent for a while. Then she said, 'Jalil-da, I think you must straightaway talk to Sajal Bose about the matter. Being the Party Chief, and being fully aware of your lifelong contribution, he should not allow this to pass. I've heard that this work has been assigned to Nalini Sen this time. You know he never writes about the real issues as you do. He only sings the Party's praises and criticizes the opposition.'

Jalil Khan was surprised. 'Has he already written, then?'

'No, not for the *Jago Samaj* as yet, but his article in *The*

Moth was highly applauded and no wonder you're being displaced. They couldn't have found a better sycophant than Nalini Sen. I think you ought to make your protest felt.'

'Jhuma, you're very bold, you mustn't talk in this manner. The Party know best in these matters and we must follow its dictum. Anyway, I've read the leaflet and I'll attend the meeting.' As the veteran closed the topic with an air of finality, Jhuma walked out of the house, infuriated.

How long would they follow the Party's dictum blindly? Repeat their meaningless utterances ad nauseum? Here, women and children are dying of hunger and disease in the bustees. No water, no sanitation, no school, no medical treatment. She had no words to offer the Sipras and Lotikas of her country. Except, *the Party knows best.*

Tanya 4

Tanya was composing an email on her laptop, in her hostel room, at a university campus in Delhi.

Dear Muru,

I hope Kancha is a little better. I consulted Dr Thakur about the enzyme injection. He said they should be administered twice a week for the next six months. I have bought four from my scholarship money and Sanjana has sponsored two. We are sending these through Ayesha. I spoke to Professor Desai yesterday and he has already issued a notice asking for contributions from the department. Most probably we will be able to raise the money for the rest of the course by April end. Then the next lot of injections will be sent to you either through courier, or if that's not allowed, Vivek will hand them over to you at Coimbatore station. Don't worry, it will be taken care of.

What about Jhimli? Did you take her to Madurai for her eye surgery? I heard from Vivek that her granddaughter has had a baby. Do let me know all the news.

I was thrilled to get your email from your battery-operated computer. Sanjana says that you were born to be an engineer, but I don't think so. I can't imagine you in one of those sanctified holier-than-thou institutions.

I am leaving for Auckland in a week's time, on the fifth of May. There are a thousand and one things to do before that. The last chapter of my project paper is still being composed. Then there are umpteen number of medical tests that I have to undergo before leaving. My MA certificates have to be collected from the university. But thankfully my visa interview has gone through and I have cleared that hurdle.

Anyway, keep me up-to-date about things at your end.
I will write again.
Bye,
Tanya

***

A month later...

Every morning, Tanya took the bus to the 'School for Maori and Pacific Studies'. Her supervisor James Henare was distant kin to the famous Maori politician of the nineteenth century, Apirana Ngata. Along with three other successful Maori politicians—James Carroll, Te Rangi Hiroa and Maui Pomare—he took the lead for revitalization of the Maori people after their steady decline in the previous century. Known as the 'Young Maori Party' the group aimed for Maori assimilation by adopting Western education and medicine. Tanya learnt that Ngata however played a special role in reviving traditional arts like the *khapahaka*, a performance art preserved since the Maoris migrated from Polynesia in thirteenth century CE.

Tanya was one among a handful of non-Maori people at her institute. She missed home but work at the institute was getting exciting. The orientation programme was over and her coursework was in full swing. The faculty was helping her to profile her plans and objectives for the coming term. For her term paper, Professor Sacha had asked her to analyse and critique existing development models for indigenous people. Keeping in mind the parallel study of the Nilgiri tribes, she had already made some forays into a Maori village. She had one or two interesting encounters with rural Maori folk right in the interiors of the *marae*, the central meeting place of a traditional Maori village. Tanya wished to understand how the Maoris had managed to assimilate themselves with the larger society while undergoing a cultural revival. As in the case of the Nilgiri tribes in India, the British colonial powers had confiscated large tracts of Maori land resulting in a complete breakdown of the tribal structure. The Treaty of Waitangi signed by the Maori tribes in 1840 guaranteed Maoris property rights in lieu of accepting British sovereignty. But this treaty was completely violated by the colonial power later as iwi land was purchased by the British. So communal ownership of land in the tribal structure gave way to individual wealth accumulation. However, from the mid-1960s, there began a growing activism to negotiate with the government to redress these injustices and return the land. Tanya thought that she must get an in depth understanding of this protest movement if she and Murugan were to achieve the same degree of success for resettling the Nilgiri tribals in their own God given land. However, her supervisor had cautioned her against chasing red herrings at this stage.

It was a forty-minute drive. As she settled herself in the bus, the cool air from the window fanned her face. She started imagining the morning scene at home. Amma would be busy preparing breakfast while Dadi read the Bangla newspaper, scanning the political news to the last detail. Clad in her starched sari, its folds falling crisply in place, her tiny silver wristwatch glittering on her slim fair hands, Dadi would be sitting erectly waiting for breakfast—the spitting image of the ancient dowager. Grandy used to say with a wink, 'Tanya, have you read the story of the Beauty and the Beast? Can you say who's who between your Dadi and me?'

Tanya's mind went back to happier times. Dadi was strictly in favour of the old loyalists and believed the new political regime to be a party of hoodlums. Dada would let drop his own comments in favour of the ruling party in a half-jesting tone. Tanya would join Dada's side with some sardonic comments, and the arguments would erupt into a full-scale war. It always ended with Ammu yelling at her to stop talking nonsense and getting down to her studies. Then she would reprimand her mother-in-law. 'I really don't understand, Ma. Why do you give Tannu this opportunity to tickle you!'

Dadi, hurt and offended, nevertheless quick to rise to the defence of her opponent, would say: 'Oh Rina, she's my own flesh and blood and I don't grudge her a good laugh. You stay out of this grandmother-granddaughter fight.'

***

When Tanya reached her institute desk and put on her computer, there was an email from Murugan. The enzyme injections seemed to be working. Kancha had got through the first part of the treatment. Muru had negotiated with the Tribal Welfare Department to acquire a fifteen-acre piece of land in Ootacamund on the outskirts of the Toda area. Once they got the land, he would spearhead a farming project for tribal agriculture. He had already spoken to the Ministry of Agriculture to provide them subsidies on seeds, manure and pesticides for growing tribal medicinal plants. He had also applied for an UGC grant to provide him with two research workers to collect the data and record facts pertaining to tribal medicinal knowledge.

Tanya's face flushed in excitement as she read Murugan's mail. He said however there was a lot of work to be done in the area of recording tribal folklore.

'Don't give up heart, Muru. I'll join you some day and we'll work hand in hand to make it the biggest ever success.'

Angela 4

Angela stared at the baby feeding at her breast. 'My baby! Will she ever call me *Mama*?' The doctors could not promise much. Fresh tears began to run down her already tear-smeared face. The counsellors had used terms like 'differently-abled' and 'challenged' to describe her baby.

Dr Luthra had spoken a lot. She had counselled her on the challenges of bringing up a child suffering from Down's syndrome. Her baby had forty-seven chromosomes instead of the normal forty-six. This changed the way the brain and body developed. Such children had to be taken for periodic tests to detect health problems. Children with Down's syndrome often suffered from heart, intestine, ear or breathing problems. But they could all be treated. Angela should not expect her to speak and walk and play in the way normal children do. Each of these activities would require untiring efforts and patience on the mother's part. But she should remember that her child could feel the same emotions as other children did. She would need a lot of love and in turn begin to demonstrate her own love for the people around her. But—Dr Luthra had cautioned Angela—she should not protect her child overmuch. Let her learn to be a self-respecting and independent individual.

Marc had refused to meet the counsellor at first. In fact, he did not even come to see the baby after the first shocking day when they learnt that she had given birth to a disabled child. At the nursing home, she would wait for Marc to come and console her. She wanted to hear him say that they were together in this. Marc had always wanted the 'best'. Had she let him down on this? Was it her fault?

The paediatrician suspected that it was a case of Down's syndrome soon after birth. But the hospital said that it could be confirmed after two weeks when the report of the blood test arrived. For Angela, the period of waiting was the worst she ever faced in her life. And there was no one to share her agony. Marc went away on a business trip to Australia three days after their child's birth.

After Dr Luthra examined her baby for the typical symptoms associated with Down's syndrome, she called the parents to her clinic at the hospital to prepare them for such an eventuality. She said that it was a lifelong condition, but with care and support, children can grow up to have healthy happy productive lives. At this point, Marc stood up. Holding the door half-open, he turned to the doctor and said loudly, menacingly, 'Don't you dare give me all that hogwash! The whole lot of you have pulled a fast one on me. Why didn't the tests that you did on her before the baby was born show it? I'll tell you why! Because you want my money. You've cheated me. But remember, Doctor, Marc Robinson is no fool. That ugly warped bundle ain't no child of mine! And I won't be saddled with it. *Not me!*' Marc slammed the door of the doctor's clinic.

Completely bewildered by this turn of events, Angela ran behind Marc on the hospital floor, imploring him, 'Marc, don't leave me. Please don't go away. Baby Mamma is *our* child; yes Marc, born out of our love for each other. She's ill but if we love her and care for her, she'll love us back.' Before the pool of gaping staff nurses, Marc thrust out his hand and pushed her away. 'Throw away that dirty bundle and come home alone if you must. I'm not taking in any diseased child.'

After a fortnight's stay in the hospital, Angela came home alone with the baby. Her parents wanted her to stay with them but she had refused. Marc was not yet back from his business trip. He had not bothered to call or communicate with her in any way in the last two weeks. However, she still hoped that he would reconcile himself to his child's plight once he was back. A tight feeling gripped Angela's throat. But as she looked at the child lying trustingly in her arms, the muscles of her face relaxed. A soft smile played on her lips. 'My baby Mamma,' she whispered, 'my own Mamma.'

***

After Angela got over her first shock, she registered herself at the IDAC (Institute for the Differently Abled Child). Here, each participant mother had to take on the responsibility of training and nurturing a child other than her own. Moreover, she was not allowed to interfere in the training of her own child which was taken up by someone else. The institute had acquired wide recognition owing to the dynamic personality of Mrs Khastagir, the founder member and chairperson. The institute provided professional and specialised courses for its mother participants.

That morning, as she was tending to Chen in one corner, her heart gave a leap. There was a thud sound. She looked up to see Sonia, her daughter, had fallen sideways and was yelling with rage and vexation. Sonia's mentor Seema had thrown the bunch of coloured non-toxic keys just out of her reach to encourage Sonia to reach out for them. As Angela turned sideways to look at Sonia crying, her heart yearned to gather her child in her arms, to comfort and cradle. But just in time she caught Sister Jose's warning look and held herself back. The rules of the institute were clearly laid out: as a mother she could not interfere with her own child's mentoring.

Instead, Angela turned to Chen whose fingers had just mastered the art of grasping the ball and throwing it. Every time Chen let the ball go, '*Oi, Oi*,' he gurgled aloud in happiness. It had taken them the labour of two months to achieve this, an act that other children of four perform effortlessly. They had toiled at it every day, the child and the adult bonded by a common sorrow. Soon Angela caught in her ward's joy forgot her own pain. She lifted Chen up and, giving him the warmest of cuddles, threw the ball back at him.

Towards the end of the day, there was a Child Progress Meet with Mrs Khastagir, where each participant reported the CP to her and discussed their lesson plans for the following week. After this, Angela got ready to go home with Sonia who jumped into her lap gurgling and cooing at the sight of her mother.

Jhuma 5

When Jhuma entered the cool interior of the District Literacy Office, she was almost wet with perspiration. The sun was blazing outside and a horrid torpor reigned over the April sky. She quickly wiped her face with a fresh hanky, and ran her hands over her hair where a few strands of hair had escaped loose from her plait. Then she headed straight towards Debasish Karmakar's cabin.

As she entered, Debasish, who was speaking to someone on his land phone, motioned her to take a seat. After he kept the receiver down, he turned towards Jhuma with a smile.

'Hullo Jhuma, I was expecting you. You look tired. Was the Burdwan Local very crowded?'

Then he rang the bell and a peon appeared. 'Bring a glass of cool water for Didi.' The peon nodded his head and then scratching his head hesitantly, uttered:

'Sir...'

'Yes, Ramcharan, what is it?'

'Sir, as you know... I have to leave early today. Nitai and Sadashiv have already left...'

'Okay, you serve the tea and then you can leave. Abani Babu will lock up and take the keys home.'

Then he turned towards Jhuma. 'Yes Jhuma, you were saying something...'

'Debasish-da, today the Burdwan Local was extremely crowded. There was hardly any standing room—I wonder why, because these were not office rush hours.'

'Today is Jamai-Shashti, don't you know Jhuma? Most of the men have taken half-day leave and are rushing to their in-laws' place. Of course, how would you know; it's not time for your parents to celebrate 'son-in-law' day as yet. So! Any interesting youngsters in sight?'

'Oh, come on, Debasish-da, you're joking as usual. Is that why the office looks so empty?'

'Yes, half the people have not come in at all and most of the others will leave at lunch. My wife was fuming because I have come to work today. She just called up to ask when I could be expected. Apparently, all the other sisters and their husbands have already assembled at her parents' place for the grand feast.'

'Oh, then you must be in a hurry. Is that why you're all dressed up in these kurta-pyjamas?'

'Yes, is this colour nice?' Debasish pointed to his embroidered silk kurta. My in-laws have bought this from Anushkka, a fashion designer in Delhi.'

'Oh, yes. It's lovely. Did Bithi-di call up to tell you that I would be bringing a draft of the poster that I designed? Here it is. Have a look and tell me whether you like it.'

Jhuma took out the artwork from her cloth bag and unrolled it before Debasish.

Debasish took out his reading spectacles and looked at it carefully. 'Yes, it is nice, Jhuma. The only change that I think would improve it is we could have the children in the foreground; and the lettering could be in a script font, instead of the handwriting. We need to print at least a lakh for World Literacy Day.'

'Oh Debasish-da, I'm so worried. I heard that the CM will be declaring that Burdwan has achieved one-hundred per cent literacy since the Saksharata drive was initiated by us. And he will also be touring the literacy centres and all this will be shown on TV. Is that true?'

'Of course, it's true. But why are you worried? There are no issues at all.'

'No issues at all? But I myself have travelled to most of the centres for neo-literates and none of the peasants or labourers' wives and children are going to these centres. No classes have been held there for the past one and a half years. We are going to claim that our three-year drive has successfully eradicated illiteracy. But what if the opposition finds out the real thing? The Greens and Oranges are going to cry foul.'

'Jhuma, you're the limit. Leave all these worries to experienced people like us. Nobody's going to find out anything. On the red-letter day, the CM will be seen visiting the centres, and don't you worry, dear, those places will be swarming with adult neo-literates. We will be printing 5000 copies each of forty-five titles. The publishers will be happy, they will get massive orders; the people will be happy to see our state ahead in the grassroot educational sphere. And there you are. What do you have to worry about?'

'And what if the media there asks any of the farmers to read from the books heaped there? They will not be able to read a word.'

'Who told you they will not be able to read a word? They will read fluently like you and I would.'

'How is that possible?'

'Silly girl! Do you think we will be so foolish as to bring the actual peasants and labourers and make them face the TV cameras? Dear lady, our cadres will be there posing as neo-literates. And mind you, do you know what will be the result of all this? As the world will be watching the event, our friends at the centre will perforce have to part with more and more funds to aid our state's literacy drive, so that we can repeat the same performance in the rest of the districts.'

Jhuma was too stunned to answer. She sat quietly for a while and finally said softly, 'Will this really benefit the people, I wonder!'

'Jhuma dear, don't worry your pretty head about all this. As I said, leave it to people like Bithi-di and me. We are pretty secure as far as the vote bank is concerned. We will again come back with a thumping majority; I can tell you that.'

'I'm sure you can,' said Jhuma quietly as she got up to leave.

Tanya 5

Tanya looked out of the window of her apartment block in Wordsworth Street. It was snowing heavily... she had been in New Zealand for a year, but never had it snowed like this. She turned up the heater a bit and made herself a big mug of coffee. Sundays were the loneliest. Not much to look forward to except the long week looming ahead. Work was all right. One of her papers on the Maoris and the Todas had been published in a prestigious tribal journal. She was working with four other students under their supervisor Mr Mason for their PhDs.

She missed home a lot. Ammu and Abbu were planning to come for a holiday last summer, but Dadi suddenly had a stroke and was now bedridden. So, they couldn't leave Kolkata even for a short while. Her heart ached to think that her proud elegant grandmother was now in bed, dependent on others for every little thing. How she must be hating that!

She was out of touch with Murugan. Their correspondence had become less and less frequent. For the first three months she was too busy adapting to life here; he was busy with the farming projects that he had undertaken for the tribals. He was trying to put on record all the varieties of plants that the Nilgiri tribals used for their medicinal purposes. She knew that it was rather tough on him doing it all alone and he had really looked to Tanya for support in his project.

The last time he had written to her about two years ago, he

had described how the procedures for the land earmarked for the project was getting inordinately delayed through red tape. She could sense his frustration in the emails when he recounted the indifference of the officials concerned.

Tanya remembered her stiff replies, the words sounding so hollow when she wrote back enquiring whether she could help him from Auckland. He didn't reply to that but after a long time she got an email: it seemed the government was considering giving the land to an industrialist for developing roads, housing estates and shopping malls there. Some of the ruling party leaders were strongly in its favour as the whole place would get connected with the main urban centre. They also felt it would result in economic development of the area by providing jobs to the tribal youth.

After that, Murugan's emails stopped coming altogether, though Tanya had written to him a number of times enquiring of his whereabouts.

Meanwhile, she had met Cliff. He had first come as Visiting Professor to their department at the institute. She remembered the first time she went to meet him in his office at the institute, she had an uncanny feeling of having done it before. She would have dismissed it as just one of those things, except for his sudden remark echoing her own thoughts. She clearly remembered the moment she entered his room... he had been sitting at his desk rearranging some of his books on a shelf behind him. He had his back towards her and for some seconds she was not sure whether he was aware of her presence. But when he finally turned round to face her, there were two things that impacted her; one, his shock of brown hair that fell across his forehead; and second, his words: 'We've met before?' Even while he uttered it both of them knew that the question needed no answer, for at no point in their lives did their paths cross. Cliff was born of Hungarian parents who had migrated to West Germany in their early life where Cliff was born. He went to college in England but went back to work in Hungary for his PhD thesis and later settled in England as part of the Faculty in the University of Cambridge. Tanya had found out the details of his childhood years, and about his youthful experiences in Hungary much later, but she was aware of his career graph even then through the department's news bulletin.

So, the answer that she had given him then remained distinct in her mind: 'Yes, there's a feeling of déjà vu, isn't there? I can only attribute it to that.'

And he replied: 'Yes, because we never met either at any of the seminars and workshops that I attended either in this part of the world nor in Singapore or Hong Kong.'

Somehow that first conversation stuck a chord with them. He was well-read, sensitive, with a great sense of humour. One Friday morning he asked her if she would like to see a dubbed version of the Indian play *Charandas Chor* directed by the playwright Habib Tanveer on Saturday evening. They had dinner after that at a Mexican restaurant. He liked poetry and one weekend she organised a cosy poetry-reading sessions for some of her friends and colleagues who had the same interests. He came in bringing his own collection written during his student years when he roamed Hungary, Rumania and what was then called Yugoslavia. Sometimes they went to different art galleries to see exhibitions of paintings.

When he went to her apartment, he was struck by the abstract painting of Ganesh Pyne and the nudes of Bikash Bhattacharya paintings in her bedroom. 'I've seen Hussain. His horse series is fantastic. I also bought a Raja Ravi Verma and a Tagore sketch at an auction house in Paris. But I had no idea of the Bengali contemporary greats.'

After some time, he moved in with her. The first few months were good, but slowly Tanya began to realise that he was just using her to get back at his wife. She had been deceiving him for a long time and when he found her out, he had moved away to Auckland. He had merely flirted with Tanya on the rebound and was now looking for a patch-up with his wife. Besides, Tanya also realised that beneath his polished exterior he was a very indolent and selfish person. Soon Tanya too began to tire of him and they decided to split.

After that it had been lonely—the weekends stretching out endlessly.

Angela 5

Cradling Sonia in one hand, Angela gingerly opened the door with her flat's key. Then she washed and fed her daughter and put her to sleep. After this, she had a bath, put on her nightgown, laid the table for two and put the food in the microwave. Tired out, she put her feet up on the sofa and waited for Marc. His flight was due to arrive at eight p.m. Suddenly her phone rang.

'Hullo.'

'Hullo Angy, I won't be back tonight.'

'Oh Marc! When will you come?'

'My work here'll take a couple of days more. The deal hasn't been finalised as yet.'

'The house seems lonely without you. But I'll manage. Take care.'

'Bye.'

***

Angela sat before Mrs Khastagir, her face white with shock as she related the previous day's happenings to her. She knew her parents wouldn't be able to cope with it and so she turned to the only person she knew who could offer her guidance.

There was a call from Marc's office that day: they couldn't reach him on his cell phone and were enquiring whether she could help them. So, she looked her mobile to locate the number from where he had called up the previous day. She guessed it would be past midnight in Washington and was undecided as to whether she should disturb him so late at night. But on a hunch, she called up and a sleepy female voice picked up the phone. At first Angela thought she had made a mistake or Marc must have moved off elsewhere. But as soon as she asked for Marc, she could hear the woman clearly saying: 'It's for you, Marc.' Angela hung up. After that Marc had called up a number of times, telling her that it was not what she assumed, there was a mistake... but Angela had refused to speak.

Mrs Khastagir listened patiently. Then she said, 'Angela, I understand what you're going through. But before we think of other alternatives, you must decide once and for all whether you really want to opt out of this relationship. The last time it happened when you had arrived unexpectedly at the airport to give Marc a surprise, he had come in holding another woman in his arms. As I understand there have been other instances too when his behaviour has aroused your suspicion. So far you have reconciled yourself by justifying them as much as possible.'

'Yes, Mrs Khastagir, but no longer can I ignore what is clear evidence of Marc's unfaithfulness.'

'So, what do you want to do?'

'I want to make a clean break and move out of his life with Sonia. For this, I need to earn my living, find an apartment for us. But the honorarium that I receive here won't be enough to sustain me and my baby.'

'Why, you can claim a fat alimony from Marc.'

'No, I won't touch his money.'

Mrs Khastagir remained in silent thought for some time. Then she looked up at Angela as if she had come to some decision. 'Okay Angela, if you're really serious, I can suggest a course of action. One of our new donor agencies has an office in the United States. They wish to fund a similar project as ours in South India and they're looking for a trained person from our end who can set up the unit in Chennai. You have gathered considerable experience in your years here and could be well suited to do this job. I am required to go to Sweden for a two-week period in order to discuss the project. If you are interested, as soon as I come back, you can fly to the US for the three-month training required to head the institute. Sonia can accompany you and stay at a crèche nearby while you are at work. We'll make arrangements for that.'

Tears filled Angela's eyes. 'Mrs Khastagir, I don't know how to thank you…'

'It's okay, child. You must be very strong in this crisis and take control of your life. And you must file a divorce case against Marc before you leave. I understand your sentiments for not wanting Marc's money. But we must nevertheless be practical and press for maintenance for Sonia, at least. You mustn't let sentiments cloud your reason because she has a rightful claim, after all.'

'Okay, Mrs Khastagir, I'll follow your suggestion. Now I must go and break the news to my parents. And then start making arrangements for a lawyer and all.'

'Why don't you request Lily Sen, one of our own participant-mothers to suggest the name of a lawyer? She comes from a lawyer's family and her husband has a firm of his own.'

'Oh yes, I'll ask Lily. Thank you, Ma'am, I'll take your leave now.'

'Bless you, my child.'

Jhuma 6

Jhuma flung the newspaper before Kishore. 'You'll claim that it is a bourgeoise newspaper. I agree. But can you deny the facts? Look at the sequence of events. Just two days before his death, Mahato Majhi gave a statement to the effect that he had the evidence to prove that two of the Panchayat members were involved in financial wrongdoings. Soon after this, Majhi and Uma Shankar were burnt alive in Majhi's house. The police claim that they were involved in bomb-making activities and were storing inflammable goods. The Greens are saying that one of our workers torched down Majhi and Uma's house. If the police knew all along that they were involved in bomb-making activities, why didn't they take any action? And who with some common sense would believe that the two houses separated by half a dozen other houses would succumb to the same accident at the same time?'

Kishore interrupted Jhuma's steady flow with his hands held up. 'Oh, shut up. Jhuma, you know nothing about these matters. The Press comes up with some voodoo theory and you fall for it. Both Majhi and Uma were in the midst of their bomb-making activities when the accident took place in Majhi's place. The houses didn't burn down at the same time. It was only later in the evening when Uma's child was playing with firecrackers—it being the eve of Kali Puja—that their house went up in flames. In the second case, all the family members were rescued.'

'Oh, how convenient,' spoke out Jhuma. 'You know as well as I do that those incriminating documents had been kept hidden in Uma's house... and of course the family members would be rescued because by then Uma and Majhi had both been eliminated.'

Kishore looked disgusted. 'The Police Commissioner himself has given the statement that the police have records of the bomb-making activities of Uma and Majhi.'

Jhuma turned towards Kishore with a look of helplessness. 'Kishore-da, I really can't understand why you can't accept the facts staring you in the face. Only if we protest against these can we stem the rot, root out the evil and cleanse the system. It's our duty to restore the party to its healthy functioning, based on the principles in which we believe.'

Just then, Bithi Sen entered the room and interrupted Jhuma's voluble discourse with a frown on her face. 'I think, Miss Sanyal, you can leave such important matters of party ideology to our senior revered members who have devoted a whole lifetime to its study. Kishore, you and I have to do the duties assigned to us. As you know, for the moment we are committed to addressing the issue of Dengue at our next WGM. The hospitals have to be notified and leaflets issued.'

Jhuma began, 'Bithi-di, I think...'

Bithi Sen put up her hand to silence her. 'Jhuma, you better look to the posters that have to be drafted, designed and put up.'

Jhuma nodded her head in stern assent while Bithi Sen issued a string of instructions.

Tanya 6

As Tanya entered his room, Dr Mason's face lit up with a smile. 'Congratulations, Tanya, you've completed your PhD with credit and your external has awarded you an A+. I wish to discuss the matter with you. You must have seen the ads put up on our campus notice-boards. There is a vacancy for a teaching assignment at the University of Pennsylvania and the other at the University of Louisiana.'

'Yes, Dr Mason.'

'So, have you started processing the applications? I see a bright future for you there.'

'Yes, but... my research has its relevance here and in India... of course; I can perhaps... put it to good use... in India.'

'I really don't know what you're getting at, Tanya. Though I teach here, we all know the research facilities at Auckland can't hold a candle to Penn. And India? Are you out of your mind? Which University of India will provide you the kind of funds that you'd get in the US to continue your post-doctoral work?'

'Well... but perhaps... the tribals in India would benefit more if I...'

'You must decide whether you want to work with the tribes or on them. There are enough NGOs being floated every day to work in the remote areas of India—our university as you know funds several of them. But your specialised knowledge, the painstaking research that you have done would have no worth if you didn't impart it to your students.'

'Yes, I suppose…'

'Don't suppose, Tanya. Come to your senses and apply. Meanwhile, get your documents ready to obtain a US visa.'

'Thank you, Dr Mason,' said Tanya as she hastily departed from her supervisor's room.

Angela 6

Angela stared out of the window of the plane as Sonia slept peacefully in her lap. She remembered the day when Marc and she had flown to Spain for their honeymoon. It had all seemed so perfect and she was ecstatic with joy. Now those memories seemed to belong to a past life. Her understanding of life had undergone a lot of change. She realised that her parents had brought her up to believe that the possession of a rich, good-looking husband, lovely children, a beautiful house, silks and diamonds were enough to make one happy.

No, she did not blame Marc for straying from her. He too, she understood now, held the same beliefs as her parents. They were uncomfortable with anything that did not match up to this idyllic picture of life, and Sonia was an imperfection that they could not bring themselves to accept. Although Angela had been brought up with the same beliefs, she had accepted this reality with a far greater graciousness than her husband and her parents. Angela knew that it was not her motherly instinct alone that prompted her to rise to the occasion. Once she moved out of her parents' household, she realised that she was intrinsically different from both them and Marc. She did not care from the core of her heart for any of the status symbols that were essential to them for their survival. Perhaps Marc too had sensed this and they had moved away from each other, and the chasm widened day by day. By being unfaithful to her, Marc had been merely true to his inner self.

As Angela looked at the sleeping figure of Sonia, she knew that, hard as it was to accept the disability that so marred her daughter's life, it had helped her to feel the pain and sorrow of human life that lay beyond the pale of the cloistered existence that was once hers. She felt an inner urge to reach out and bond with the sufferings of other men and women.

Suddenly Sonia woke up and began to cry. 'Yes, I know it's time for your feed, dear.' She took out the sealed can of baby food that she was carrying and called for the airhostess to heat it. On the aisle seat next to Angela sat a young lady from the subcontinent with a fair complexion and short wavy hair that curled over her cheeks. She was immersed in a book titled 'A Deconstruction of Tribal Savagery'. But when Baby Mamma started crying, the lady turned towards Angela with a smile. 'It looks like your daughter is hungry.'

Angela smiled in reply. 'Yes, I'm sorry for the racket she's making. It must have disturbed you.'

'Oh, no, it's perfectly fine. She's a charming baby.'

When the airhostess brought in the food, the lady turned towards Angela and asked her if she could help out. So, while Sonia sat comfortably on her mother's lap, the lady fed her with a spoon. When she finished eating, the little baby gurgled happily and smiled at her neighbour. Angela said, 'Now Mamma, you must thank Aunt…'

'Aunt Tanya,' smiled the young lady.

'And I'm Angela,' said the baby's mother. 'I'm traveling from Kolkata to Pennsylvania. Are you an Indian?'

'Yes, I'm from Kolkata too, but I was in New Zealand for my PhD. I went to Singapore to attend a conference. And now I am on my way to Penn for my post-doctoral work. Are you going to the US as a tourist or for work?'

'Yes, in a way for work. I'm going for a three-month training programme. After that, I come back to India to work in an NGO for differently-abled children. Sonia will stay in the crèche during the day. It's good to hear that you are going to Pennsylvania too. This will be my first visit to the US.'

'Same here. Can I take your address and phone number so that we can keep in touch with each other?'

'Oh, thanks Tanya, that would be wonderful.'

***

The bell rang. Tanya rushed to open the door. She could hear Sonia's chirpy voice outside. As she hugged Angela, the child cried out 'Auntie' and put her arms out towards Tanya. 'Oh, my Baby Mamma, come.'

The two friends would meet invariably on weekends and other holidays. Angela was enjoying her work and the bonding with Tanya gave her a deep sense of security. For Tanya, too, this companionship with Angela and little Sonia's deep affection for her meant a lot.

After they had settled down, Angela made two big mugs of coffee in Tanya's neat kitchen and got ready for a hearty chat. Meanwhile, Tanya made Baby Mamma comfortable by making her sit on a mat surrounded by cushions, books and toys and switching on her favourite cartoon channel.

Tanya was extremely disturbed by a phone call that she had received from Sanjana early that morning. It was a relief to have

Angela to share the news with. She related her friendship with Murugan. Skirmishes had now broken out between the Kotas and the Badagas. Although Murugan had advocated the Kotas to wait for the court verdict about the decision regarding the ownership of their land, a group of Kotas had been instigated by the opposing political party to adopt violent means. Tanya was worried how this would affect Murugan.

Angela suggested that Tanya should try calling up Murugan to enquire.

After trying a number of times, Murugan came on the line. He told Tanya that it was true that a group of the Kotas had been misled and resorted to violence. But since then, Murugan had been incessantly holding meetings to explain matters to them. The situation had improved and matters were now almost under control. So, there was not much cause to worry.

Tanya then told Murugan that a friend of hers who was also an Indian would like to speak to him. Angela introduced herself to Murugan and told him about the kind of institute that they were planning to set up in Chennai. Murugan replied saying that there would definitely be a need for that kind of an institute in the tribal areas that he planned to demarcate especially for the Nilgiri tribes around Ooty as many of the tribal children were born with physical disabilities due to the in-breeding practices prevalent there. Angela said that she would contact Mrs Khastagir and see if it was possible to have a centre exclusively for the tribal children in that area. Meanwhile, she suggested that Murugan should send a written proposal to Mrs Khastagir identifying the special need there.

After the phone call. Tanya fed Sonia her meal while Angela made another call to Mrs Khastagir and told her about her conversation with Murugan. Mrs Khastagir promised to look into the matter once Murugan's email reached her.

Later in the evening the two went out to shop for groceries and then Tanya drove Angela and Sonia home. The child kissed her Aunt Tanya goodbye as she got out from the car.

Jhuma 7

Jhuma hurriedly scanned the old dusty files in the large cupboard in the Party Office. Most of the leaders and Party workers were attending the mass meeting in front of the Shahid Minar. She had quietly slipped out and made her way back knowing that she would not get a more opportune moment to hunt the files. The old clerk Abani Babu had given her the key when she told him that Sudhir Bose had asked her to fetch an important document.

Each page was divided into neat columns. The farmer's name was written on the first column. *Moinuddin Sheikh, Golambajar North, 6 katha @Rs 15000 Total sum paid Rs 90,000/; Jasmuddin Rahman, Golambajar North, 3 katha@Rs15000 Total sum paid Rs 45,000;* Jhuma turned to the middle pages: *Rakhal Biswas, Golambajar South East,10 katha, @Rs 20000 Total sum paid Rs 200000/; Sumanto Sanyal, Golambajar South East, 7.5 katha @ 20000/ Total sum paid Rs 150000/.* Jhuma glanced through the list of 1500 names as quickly as she could. In between there was a memo okaying the purchase of land at Golambajar from farmers at the rate of Rs 15000-20000 per katha as per location.

Jhuma seethed with rage: all this exploitation and oppression in the name of development. Some of these farmers had complained to Manisha, one of Jhuma's closest friends among the Party cadres, that Sudhir Ghosh was threatening to wrestle their land forcibly from them if they did not take the price offered. But she must tread very cautiously and discuss matters with Kishore before taking any steps. She quickly photocopied the relevant documents, locked the cupboard, returned the key to Abani Babu and quickly went out.

As she entered the meeting ground, she could hear the voice of Sudhir Bose addressing the crowd of people: 'Dear Comrades, this is the time to break free of your shackles and unite to claim your legitimate rights…'

After the meeting was over, Jhuma told Kishore that she needed to speak to him. They both went to the culvert on the marsh and sat down. Jhuma told Kishore about Manisha's chat with the farmers in which she got to know that they had sold their land perforce to the government at very low rates on threats of oppression. To verify the truth, she had made some secret explorations of the Party files that afternoon.

'What you've done is wrong! It's against our Party rules. Do you know the amount of risk you've taken?'

'I've told you before I've never cared for risks. And you're saying what I did was wrong! Wrong! Who's wronging whom? Please come to your senses, Kishore-da. Get yourself out of this blind obedience for the Party and do right by the People. It's a People's Party and here we are extorting them, oppressing them.'

'Come on, you can't come to such conclusions without verifying the truth of it.'

'That's exactly what I'm asking you to do, but let's at least give truth a chance.'

'Sure. I'm all for it. Let's call Manisha here and find out what has been revealed to you.'

They were sitting on the culvert where Jhuma had sat with Kishore long back, expressing her wish to serve the Party. As evening fell, droves of mosquitoes gathered around them. The croaking of frogs in the shadows beat a monotonous rhythm and filled the air with a nostalgia for innocence lost. It seemed aeons back when she had cherished such a romantic notion of the Party.

'Kishore-da, we must do something to reveal the truth. Look, I've got photocopies of all the documents.'

After Kishore read the documents, he bowed his head in silence. 'Yes, we must do something about this. But we have to be very careful. Ask Manisha to come here. I want to know the facts from her.'

***

From a distance they could see Manisha's shadowy figure coming towards them on the bridge across the marsh and the heaviness of her tread suggested that she was tired after the day's events. As she came within eyesight, Jhuma could make out that weary as she was, she was still looking lovely in a cotton printed brown Orissa kotki sari with a navy-blue border and a matching blouse. Unlike the rest of the cadres, men and women alike, Manisha never carried one of those shabby cloth jholas. The bag that hung on her shoulder was of the voluminous designer bags made of Shantiniketan leather which one got to see only in boutiques. Plump as she was, her sari suited her admirably well though her hair was ruffled and strands of it had come loose from the neat pony tail into which she usually tied her hair.

'What, Jhuma? Why this urgent summons? Hi, Kishore da! You are here too. What a surprise!'

'Hi Manisha! You must be tired after the meeting. What was your role in it?' asked Kishore.

'Yes, I am dead tired,' said Manisha as she settled herself comfortably on the culvert between Jhuma and Kishore. 'I was returning home to Salt Lake when Jhuma's call came.

'My role? I was supposed to drag out all the people from the Rampurhat area in Birbhum district and get them to Kolkata for the rally. So yesterday I took the 5.15 a.m. Rampurhat local and made all the arrangements, came back by the Shantiniketan express in the evening and went straight to the Party office. This morning I got up early and boarded the local buses reserved for the Party and brought around 150 people to the city. Took them first to the zoo and from there on to the Indian Museum. Then I distributed their biriyani packets and finally took them to the rally point at Bowbajar. I had already coached them their lines, but in case they forgot, I made them repeat the slogans before the rally. After eating all that biriyani, their lung power was really strong. But I find it so contradictory. On one hand the Party is supporting the Greens at the centre from outside and within the state we are shouting silly slogans like *We cannot permit scams . . . Oppose the dirty hands of the Greens!* I'm pretty tired of all this. Anyway, what were you up to?'

'I was doing much the same as you. Rounding up people from Baruipur. And showing them around Botanics and the zoo—the zoo's a must. I myself feel like a creature belonging to it.'

'We've called you to discuss something very important,' said Kishore, turning towards Manisha. 'I notice that you kept repeating that you are tired. When you are charged with passion for a cause, one doesn't feel tired. But even Jhuma and I have been feeling this strong sense of ennui gripping us. We wanted to know certain facts from you. I believe the farmers have been talking to you.'

'Not just the farmers. Since I spoke to Jhuma, I have done quite a bit of exploration on my own.'

'Yeah, like?'

'It's a long story, but I'll try to summarise it up. First, I was casually speaking to some of the farmers in Golambajar where we have acquired their land to build New City; and what came out was pretty sad. Each flat there you know sold at prices ranging from Rs thirty to six lakhs at an average which meant, say, ten katha of land was worth a minimum of three-hundred lakhs. If the farmer had sold directly to the industrialist, he would have got at least three lakhs per katha. This would provide him some means for sustenance or he could invest in something like a shop or a trade which would provide him with a recurring income for a lifetime in lieu of his land; instead, the government pays him a paltry sum of Rs 15000-20000/. In a situation of constant want, that money is swallowed up in no time and now these farmers have neither money nor land. Is it a fair situation, tell me?'

Jhuma said, 'You know guys, I was thinking that it's a blessing for the Party that the media hasn't reached them. Otherwise, if they get wind of it, there'd be a terrible uproar and the Greens and the Oranges would surely jump into the fray.'

Kishore sat quietly for a while. Then he asked Manisha, 'What about the other things that you had referred to?'

Manisha said: 'Kishore-da, as far as those things go, I've got a better idea. It may be more convincing if you meet the people and talk to them yourselves. You know what, tomorrow in Surajpur in South Parganas, there is a village trial to be held because one man has married twice. We'll get a chance to talk to the villagers. You must hear it from them. Can you and Jhuma come over?'

'Yes, let's go,' said Jhuma to Kishore.
    'Okay,' said Kishore, 'What time?'
    'We'll meet at ten at Sealdah Station, shall we? The trial begins at two p.m. in the afternoon. The journey will take forty-five minutes to one hour. That gives us enough time to move around and talk to them. Right! I will make my move. Bye.'
    Jhuma and Kishore also got up to leave.

Tanya 7

Tanya received a call from Sanjana who was teaching in the Sociology department of Delhi University.

'...I met Murugan in the university today. He has come to Delhi to pursue the case of having an exclusive tribal domain for their cooperative farming. He came to meet Rajeevan, Sushmita and me to see if we could raise some funds to meet the expenses of the lawyer, etc. I've invited him and the others for dinner tomorrow to my house. I'll give you a call and you can talk to him then.'

'I really envy you people meeting together. What fun it would be! I feel so much of an alien here.'

'You can't have your cake and eat it too, dear. You wanted to go to the "exotic West" and that was your choice.'

Tanya was silent for a while. Then she asked,

'How is he?'

'Oh, he seems to have lost around ten kilos of weight and is looking terribly haggard.'

'Yes Sanjana, I would like to talk to him. It's been a long time since we communicated. Do you have his cell number?'

'Yes, I do. Here it is: 09822913346.'

'Good. Then I'll call him up and speak with him now. I have a faculty party tomorrow evening at a colleague's house. I'll be reaching home late and may miss the opportunity to talk. Thanks, Sanji, for letting me know.'

'Bye.'

After hanging up, Tanya began to dial Murugan's number. After trying a couple of times, Murugan's deep voice came through.

'Hullo.'

'Hullo Muru, this is Tanya.'

'Hi, how are you?'

'I am all right. How are things at your end? I believe you're having problems regarding your plans of building a cooperative in the territory of the Kotas.'

'Yes, a local industrialist group wants to build a mall and a cosmetic factory here in the land selected for the cooperative. The state government is trying to negotiate with me as the representative of the Kotas for this land. I had put an injunction and filed a case in the Tamil Nadu High Court against this. However, the High Court has overruled my objection, so I've filed a fresh case in the Supreme Court.'

'I could raise some funds from our faculty members who I think would be sympathetic to the cause.'

'Yes, that will help me to tide over the costs of the case in the Supreme Court. I am confident that we will win if we can appoint the top lawyers to fight the case. But Tanya, more importantly, you have to arrange a grant for building the cooperative on this land. I'll email you explaining the entire scheme that I've planned to develop here. I need a lot of financial support for that.'

'Okay, send me the mail and I'll see what I can do from here. Another thing, Muru, along with your work, you must take care of your health. Sanjana says you have lost a lot of weight and I can hear your racking cough. You must do something about this.'

'Don't worry about me. I'll be all right. It's the plight of those poor tribals that haunts me day and night. They are so helpless in the face of our so-called civilised society that threatens to extinguish them totally. We must do something to save them.'

'Yes, I understand, but don't overdo and don't take unwarranted risks, at least for their sake. They need you and you have to live for them. Bye.'

Angela 7

On Monday morning Angela opened her mail box to find an email awaiting her from Mrs Khastagir.

She had written to say that she had approached the funding agency of IDAC in Sweden. They approved the idea of having a free centre for tribal children in principle but the logistics needed to be worked out. One of the key questions she was faced with was: who would take the responsibility of starting the institute in Ooty as they would require a person with a background in tribal studies. Mrs Khastagir had written that there was no scope for going through the usual processes of advertising in newspapers for the right candidates and then shortlisting them for interviews and so on because the Board of Directors' meeting was due to start in two days' time. They would have to pass the resolution at that meeting as the Board was interested in expanding its operations in India. If they failed to pass Ooty as the next site at this meeting, preference would be given to Mumbai. This would set back the proposal for Ooty by five years.

As soon as Angela had finished reading the email, she asked the operator to connect her to Mrs Khastagir in Kolkata. She told the latter that she had read the mail and realised the urgency of the situation. She would get back to her by the next morning on the matter.

Twilight had deepened to dusk when Tanya met Angela at

the Café de Monico. Angela had not said much over the phone except to say that there were certain developments related to the opening of the IDAC in Coonoor which she needed to discuss urgently with Tanya. She had called in for a baby sitter for Baby Mamma for the evening. Tanya understood that it had to be something very serious to prompt Angela to leave the child at home. Tanya had a faculty meeting which ended only at six in the evening. From there, she drove straight to the café that Angela suggested would be midway for both of them.

Angela briefed Tanya about the main points of the matter as Mrs Khastagir had informed her. 'Tanya, now the whole matter rests on you.'

'On me?' Tanya looked startled.

'Of course. Where else can we find a person with a research degree in tribal studies at such short notice—and one who would be willing to relocate to Ooty which is about the back of beyond for someone with a degree like yours.'

'And what gave you the idea that I would be willing to shift to this back of beyond destination at such notice? Aren't you taking me rather for granted?'

'Come on, Tanya. I'm not doing anything of that sort. I'm merely asking you if you would be interested. Please don't be offended, but it would be such a wonderful opportunity to use the knowledge that you have acquired. Think about it. Don't just react immediately.'

Tanya sat in silence for a while with her head bowed. Then she touched Angela's hand and said, 'I'm sorry, Angela. It was I who introduced Murugan to you and it's Murugan and my vision that you are trying to fulfil by having a centre for tribal children in Ooty. I'm awfully sorry for reacting like that... it's just that I've put aeons of mental distance between me and my family, though I do think about them a lot... so the prospect of returning to India—whether it's Ooty or Kolkata, India is home—makes me feel uneasy.

Angela replied softly, 'No Tanya, you needn't say sorry to me. What are friends for? I understand how you feel about going back to India. After meeting you and having such a good time here, at first, I was also feeling a bit reluctant to go back to India. I have such unpleasant memories associated with it. But then I told myself that the service that I will do for the children there will be the rent that I pay for all the privileges that I've enjoyed as an empowered social being.'

'Wow, Angela, that's a wonderful way of looking at it!' exclaimed Tanya with admiration for her friend. 'I wish I could be half as good as you.'

'But you are. So, buck up and let's all go to India and be merry,' said Angela in a light tone. 'Seriously, we can do some really good work out there. Not that I'm implying that you're not doing so here. But I mean real work for real people who need it.'

'That's exactly what Muru used to say,' said Tanya softly.

'Did he?'

'Yes, he felt if we got together and worked for them out in the field, we could use our knowledge to prevent the larger power structures from co-opting them into the mainstream.'

'Well, all that I understand is that their children need to be taken care of, and one needs sensitivity and knowledge of their culture to work with them. You have both. So, join me,'

Tanya looked at Angela for a moment and then sat with her

head bowed silently for a while. A minute later when she looked up again Angela knew that Tanya had made up her mind.

She simply said, 'No, I need a little more time for myself. I am not yet ready to commit myself. Yet I know that I will join you and Muru one day.'

'But this may be an opportunity lost,' said Angela.

'I'm not sure I look at it that way. The role that I want to play if I ever get back to India is to support Murugan in a movement that could provide a model for the rest of the Indian tribal territories. To provide the Nilgiri tribes a way of sustaining their own way of life... through a cooperative system nurtured by them... through use of tribal medicine... revival of tribal folklore... we need to fight against the system... for that, I need to be free from any institutional shackles... I need to prepare myself...'

'Now I am beginning to understand, Tanya,' said Angela slowly, 'your dreams are far bigger.'

Suddenly, Tanya looked animatedly at Angela. 'Yes, but till then, do for him what I couldn't. I came away when he had called for my support.'

'For Muru?'

Tanya nodded.

'Are you in love with him?'

Tanya was silent for a moment, and then she replied, 'I don't know. But with his vision, certainly.'

Then the two friends made preparations to leave, both of them immersed in thoughts of their imminent parting. The friendship that had developed between the two in this short time had been deep and had served to heal some of the wounds they had received from their near ones back home. And as Angela pointed out, little Sonia would miss her aunt as much as they would miss each other's company. At the mention of Sonia, Tanya found it hard to check her tears because she knew how lonely the weekends would be once more without Sonia and Angela around to spend time with.

Jhuma 8

The local train which the three boarded at 10.24 a.m. brought them to Barinpur station in twenty minutes' time. From there, the three friends took a bus up to Surajpur. It was the last stop and the whole bus became empty. While Jhuma, Kishore and Manisha were conversing among themselves in which direction they should walk, one of the passengers who alighted from the bus asked them where they wanted to go. On hearing that they intended to go to 'Samarpur' which was a good ten to fifteen kilometres away, he told them that they should avail of the 'van-rickshaw'. The contraption to which he referred was a tiny cart attached to a cycle, which people used for commuting in these parts. The three thought it was a good idea and thanked the person. The man, clearly a local, then asked if he could also accompany them as he was going to the same place. Suspecting that he could interfere with their scheme, Kishore politely dissuaded him from doing so. Then they hired the rickshaw for the whole day and told the driver that they would stop from place to place as their work demanded.

It was the end of May and it was sweltering hot. But once the van-rickshaw started, a gentle breeze relieved them. They soon crossed the boundaries of the tiny station and came to the main path between the green fields. Rice fields filled with water lined the two sides. Men were working in the fields as they drained the fields and prepared them for the sowing. After travelling for almost fifteen minutes, they saw a tiny cluster of huts. They could see some children playing nearby. Behind one of the huts was a pond towards which some women were carrying piles of clothes and dishes for washing. Kishore asked the driver the name of the village. He said it was a Muslim village called Muhammadpur. He pointed to a large pucca building that was slightly segregated from the others and said that it was the local secondary school. Most students from surrounding villages came to study here. But apparently there was some trouble brewing because the teachers of the school had been accused of conducting terrorist activities on the sly by the Orange party a few days back. This had led to a few skirmishes between the goons of the political party and the Muslim youth. But things had quietened down due to timely intervention by the police.

Jhuma told Kishore and Manisha, 'We've got plenty of time on our hands. Shall we get down and talk to the villagers here?'

As the other two agreed instantly, they told the rickshaw driver to wait for a while on the main road. Then the three got down and started walking down the narrow path that led to the village. A farmer greeted them on the way and asked them politely whom they'd like to meet. The three introduced themselves as Party workers and said they had come from Kolkata to talk to the men, women and children. The farmer took them to the school building. Then he went in and called the headmaster out to talk to them. The man gave his class some arithmetic work to do meanwhile. He was a tall man with a beard, about forty years of age. He was wearing a cream-coloured kurta with white pyjamas and a pair of rubber sandals on his feet. The farmer who had introduced himself as Golam Hussain came forward with the school teacher and said 'This is our headmaster. Sir, these people have come to talk to us.'

The schoolmaster said, 'I am Nabi Baksh.' The he lifted his hand to do adab to all of them. After the three greeted him, he led them to a shaded courtyard of the schoolhouse. Here seats had been carved in cement for people to sit. As they seated themselves, Nabi Baksh said, 'This school building is the only pucca house you will see in the whole vicinity. The rest are all huts.'

'How many children study in your school?' asked Manisha.

'This is the only government school catering to around ten villages in the vicinity. We have a student strength of about 155-160, and most of the children travel several miles to come here.'

'Do they all walk to and fro?' enquired Kishore.

'Yes, unlike Kolkata city, they don't have buses and trams here, unfortunately. And even if they had the facility, they couldn't afford it. They barely get two decent meals a day.'

'How do the people in these parts sustain themselves? Do they cultivate enough?'

'They cultivate as much as three paddy crops round the year. These parts are washed by the tide of the Damodar tributary and the soil is very fertile. But the middlemen eat up all the profits and the cultivators are left with a bare pittance.'

Meanwhile, Golam Hussain came forward with some green coconut water for all of them. The cool salty water tasted delicious in the heat. Jhuma thought to herself that the rural poor may have little but their hospitality was all the more genuine for that.

As they sipped their coconut drink, Manisha pointed out to Nabi Baksh that she was wondering why the headmaster was taking classes. There seemed to be very few teachers in school that day. Were all the other teachers out on some special duty?

A faint smile played on Nabi Baksh's bearded face as he shook his head, it seemed as if he didn't quite know how to answer her question. Then he said softly,

'It's election time. So, most of the teachers are out canvassing for the Party. Besides, those who come in from the town arrive only after twelve noon. And they return early too because they catch the 3.10 local, to avoid the evening five o'clock rush.'

Jhuma said, 'And do they get their full pay, Sir?'

Nabi Baksh looked shocked. 'Of course, they do. They get good government scales which is way above what is paid in the privately-owned schools. But you see I have been in the teaching profession for the last eighteen years. This absenteeism is the norm in government schools in rural and urban areas rather than the exception. They know that whether they come to classes or not, they will get their pay at the end of the month. And that is all that matters. There is no conscience to speak of. But, I must say, it's extremely sad for the student... their parents send them to school with a lot of expectations. But they grow up learning almost nothing. So, who's the sufferer? Ultimately the nation. How far can it go if its grassroots pull it down?'

The three listened quietly to the headmaster. They realised that Nabi Baksh was a person who was truly dedicated to his students, and his frustration with a system that failed them was apparent.

***

Their next stop was Samarpur which took them about thirty minutes more on their van-rickshaw. This was a largish village and they could see hutments stretching out on both sides of the road. There were a number of large ponds outside the village, though the water looked very dirty and bracken. Manisha observed that generally these ponds were used for bathing the bullocks and by the menfolk too for their baths. The ponds used by the women were generally in the interior of the village. But the water that they used for their drinking purposes usually came from the same pond in which they did their washing. This led to unhygienic conditions and was often the cause of various epidemics that spread in the rural areas.

Jhuma, Kishore and Manisha came to a halt in front of a large banyan tree that stood like a sentinel guarding the village. They gave some money to the rickshaw driver to have his afternoon meal and told him to wait in the shade for a couple of hours until they returned. Many of the village children who saw them get down from the van-rickshaw crowded around them.

'Where do you want to go, Didi?' they asked Jhuma and Manisha.

They said, 'We've come to talk to you. Tell us your names.'

And the three were soon engaged in conversation with the children. When asked why they weren't in school, they replied, 'We used to go to school till last year. Six of us used to travel by a van-rickshaw. Three in front, three at the back. We learnt so many things in schools. We learnt poems and songs. We used to sing *Jana Gana Mana*. But now we don't go to school because our lands are getting sold off and we have no money left to pay for the van-rickshaw. And we have to work in the quarry.'

'Do you know why we sing *Jana Gana Mana*?'

The two boys shook their heads. One of the girls whose name was Sarama said, 'I know, Head Master told us it is our National Anthem.'

'Good,' said Jhuma. 'You must also remember that it was written by Rabindranath Tagore, our great poet who won the Nobel Prize. Now tell us what do you do the whole day if you don't go to school?'

The boys, Ramesh and Samaresh, were brothers. Ramesh said, 'We work in the quarry with our fathers. And we are helping in the construction of new buildings for New City.'

'Okay, and Sarama, what do you do?'

'I look after my younger brothers and sisters. I wash the dishes and help my mother peel the vegetables.'

'When you went to school last year, did you get the free meals that are arranged for you by the government?'

'Sometimes we got only rice without dal and vegetables. The teachers said that the dal and vegetables were spilt on the way. On some rare days, we got full meals of rice, dal, vegetable curry and curd. Then we ate a lot.'

Kishore said, 'You all are good children. Now can you show us the way to where the grown-ups are?'

The children said, 'Come with us,' and they started running towards the centre of the village.

Manisha said, 'Wait a minute,' and she called up Ram Das to whom she had spoken before. 'Ram da, we've arrived. We're just on the way to your house.'

Then she told the children to take them to Ram Das *Chashi's* house.

Jhuma, Manisha and Kishore walked the distance of a kilometre through the village path, passing by two ponds at the back of a number of huts to arrive at the house of Ram Das. Kishore said, 'Trees and water bodies make so much of a difference. It's not half as hot here due to the large number of trees here, as it was at the periphery of the village, isn't it?' Ram Das *Chashi,* or farmer, as he was popularly referred to, lived at the other end of the village. He was waiting in the courtyard of his hut and welcomed them in. Manisha introduced the other two. 'Ram-da, these are my friends, Kishore and Jhuma.' Kishore and Jhuma did namaskar with their hands joined together in a gesture of greeting.

They sat on a mat in the courtyard. His daughter brought cool green coconut water for them all to drink. The top of the green coconuts was cut out and they sipped the water from a paper straw inserted in the water.

'What is the trial about today?' asked Kishore.

Ram-da said, 'You see, Chashi Bhubon Mondol's daughter was married to one party worker who came to ask for her hand from the next village. Two years have passed since the marriage took place, but now it has come to light that he already has one wife and two sons from the previous marriage. But the boy's party alleges that the girl's father knew about him.'

Kishore said, 'Do you think he really knew about it, Ram-da?'

Ram Das lit a biri, took a deep puff and then replied gently, 'You see, brother, the people in this village are really poor, and are facing further difficulties since the government has started staking claim on their land. When it comes to one less mouth to feed, they are glad to get rid of one daughter. And sometimes for the sake of such conveniences, many facts are brushed aside. The father may know but won't reveal it even to the members of his family.'

Then Ram Das got up from his courtyard and said, 'Come with me, I'll take you to some of the Chashi brothers' houses. Then you will get to know the real story.'

They moved to the next hut where three farmers were sitting and chatting in front of their huts. Ram Das said, 'Brothers, these people are our friends who have come all the way from Kolkata to talk to us about the hardships that we face in our daily lives.'

After greeting them, Jhuma asked one of the farmers, 'Do you own any land here?'

The farmer said, 'I used to own about four kathas of land. But now I've sold them to the government.'

Jhuma said, 'Was that done of your own free will?'

The farmer said, 'Didi, when the land reforms were done by the Party in 1977, I bought them from the landlord at very cheap rates. But my land fell on the way of the New City that is being built now. So, after twenty years, the government asked me to sell the land to them. They have given me very nominal rates of Rs 20,000/ per katha. Then we had to pay taxes, etc. After that we spent a lot of money this year repairing our hut as the floods last year had affected it badly and it was in a ramshackle state. How will I sustain my whole family on this little money? This year I have to give my daughter in marriage. In villages, it is very difficult to keep a grown daughter at home. The groom's parents are asking for a dowry of Rs 20,000 cash and two tolas of gold. They have heard that I have become a rich man by selling my land. But tell me what status does a farmer have without a single katha of land to his name?'

Kishore spoke to yet another farmer. 'Tell me, Chacha, did you also dispose of your land?'

The man clad in a lungi and dirty white kurta was sitting cross-legged on the mat. His skin was tanned hard as leather and seemed to bear the testimony of generations of hard work on the fields. He pondered for a while and slowly spoke out. 'To me, dear, my land was what you children are to your parents. They were my golden lands. They had been with us for six generations or more. My great-grandfather was in the services of the Rajah of Cooch Behar. Happy with his services, he had granted him ten bighas of land in the prime area here. These lands were so fertile that if ever a person did not get enough to eat, the saying goes that they would always get a plate of rice at Bijoy Chashi's house, i.e., what my grandfather was known as. Son, you must also know this—when our great-grandfather passed on the land to his family, he enjoined on us that we must forever till the soil ourselves. So, we never became the proverbial 'zamindars' but remained mere *chashis*. As the land passed downwards in time, it became divided among the various strands of the family and the allotments got smaller and smaller with time. When it came to me, I owned five kathas. But these five kathas did not just mean an inanimate asset to me. They were like my five golden living children. Do you know they yielded four rice crops a year?

Here, the man paused and wiped his eyes.

Kishore prompted mildly, 'Chacha, did you have to sell all your land?'

'Yes, son, so that on the stilled hearts of my children, highrises can be built in which the rich will live.'

Ram Das said, 'Maybe these sisters and brother who have come to lend an ear to our woes can communicate it to their seniors and some good come out of it. Now Didi, Dada, shall we make a visit to the women's quarters so that you can hear their plight too?'

Manisha said, 'Yes, that's a good idea, Ram-da. Let's visit them in their homes.'

The three then bid everyone namaskar and was accompanied by Ram Das to one of the huts where the ladies were assembled. Kishore asked one elderly lady who was standing at the door of the hut, 'Do you mind if I too come in?' The lady answered, 'No, dear, you are like our son. Please come in and make yourself comfortable.'

Manisha, Jhuma and Kishore took off their shoes at the entrance and entered. The interior of the hut was cool and clean. There were ladies of different age groups sitting on a mat on the floor. Some small children were playing beside their mothers. The younger women had covered their heads with their sari ends.

The elderly woman who was the wife of Ram Das ushered the three in and asked them to sit on the mat. Jhuma and Manisha soon became friendly with the women, asking them their names, how many children they had and so on.

After a while, Jhuma asked one of the middle-aged women: 'You said you got your daughter married to a school teacher in the next village at the age of fifteen. But you know that in our country it is not legal for girls to get married before they are eighteen. Then why do you people not follow the law?'

The woman replied, 'Didi, it is very easy for the government to make these laws. But they are the ones who force us to break the law. Do they know what the ground reality is like? Our women are harassed day and night by the Party workers. We live in fear of them. Sometimes they snatch our young daughters from our bedsides and we watch helplessly. This young man, the school teacher who married my daughter, had the reputation of being a drunkard and a womanizer. I had no wish to have him as our son-in-law. But what can I tell you of our plight? We have six children and we can hardly cope with the expenses of providing them two square meals a day. On top of that, we were harassed by the school master and other Party workers that if we did not give our daughter in marriage to him, even this hut that we are left with would be burnt down one day. My husband said, "There would be one stomach less to feed. Give her away in marriage, at least she will get food to eat and clothes to wear." Now if they put us in jail for breaking the law, the Sarkar will have to take the responsibility of feeding us there.'

All the women began to pour out similar stories of their woes. Some said, 'Before the elections, we are delivered bundles of rice and flour free of cost. But once we have cast our votes, none care to visit and enquire whether we live or die. Now we understand the trick and don't want to vote for them anymore. But they threaten us that if we don't vote for them, they will not let us survive.'

After chatting for some time, Manisha, Jhuma and Kishore took their leave from the women. It was also time for them to catch the 4.15 local to Sealdah. Ram Das came to see them off to the place where the van-rickshaw was waiting for them. They thanked him and set off towards the station, each of them immersed in the stories of hardship and oppression that their ears had borne witness to.

Tanya 8

Tanya came back from the university after her classes, made herself a large cup of coffee and sat down to compose an email to Murugan.

Hi Muru,

How are things with you? Last week I spoke to my colleagues about the situation in your territory in India and we've have had fruitful discussions on that front. As far as the funding for your court expenses go, we've agreed to put together a regular subscription from our salary which we could send you on a regular basis. This would amount to a small sum of around $2000 a month.

However, the bigger challenge is to get adequate sponsorship to fund the cooperative scheme. After healthy debate, we decided not to go ahead with the idea of inviting corporate sponsorship sourced from some of my colleagues' husbands' multinational firms. As you pointed out initially, they'd want a bite of the cake too and would interfere with your marketing schemes.

So, our next option was to look out for NGO donors. We sounded out some who are associated with us through various projects and schemes. Genesis is one such who are also interested in doing some developmental work in India. They will provide the larger initial contribution that you need for the basic infrastructure of around $50,000. However, Genesis will *not move until all the papers are cleared by the Government of India. Till the land issue is sorted out, I suggest we send Genesis a complete project outlay which I would also like to circulate among the members of my department who are sponsoring on their own—just so that everybody is in the know and everything is above board. We will also send each and every one a financial statement, a work report and a utilization certificate every three months. Do you agree, Muru? For this, you need a secretary operating from an office. Maybe Angela can help you set up this.*

Now, Muru, let me come to another bit of crucial news. I was speaking to Amritha, you know, the colleague who also comes from Kolkata. She has a childhood friend apparently called Jhuma, whose uncle is a top-notch lawyer with the Supreme Court. But what's interesting is that he started out as a Leftist with the United Party, but he's completely disillusioned with the present regime and has fallen out with them. And what stands to our interest is that he does cases free of charge if he feels the cause is right. Amritha says that if we could approach him through Jhuma, we would be spared the enormous litigation fees and the case is bound to go in our favour.

Now, Muru, hurry up and answer this mail. I was bursting at the seams with all the news. Now I'm dying to hear what your response is going to be.

Tanya

After about two hours, Tanya's mobile started ringing. It was Murugan calling.

'Hi, Muru.'

'Hi!'

There was a pause while Tanya waited for Murugan to

collect his thoughts.

'Tanya…'

'Yes?'

'This friend of yours, Amritha. How well does she know the other girl—Jhuma?'

'Um… pretty well… I think.'

'Is her uncle, I mean Jhuma's uncle's name, Asutosh Sengupta?'

'Um… hang on, I've got it written somewhere. Yes, here it is. Asutosh Sengupta. Do you know him?'

'No, I don't. But I made enquiries and found out that AS, as he is referred to in court, is a wonder man. He fights against all kinds of injustice and wins his cases too if he sets his mind to it. We must contact him through this girl.'

'Okay. I'll tell Amritha to speak to Jhuma and then probably you could speak to her directly.'

'Okay. You do that. And let me know.'

Jhuma 9

'Kishore, do you know what happened this morning? I received a call from a friend of Amritha called Murugan. This boy is doing some splendid work among the Nilgiri tribes.'

'Oh, that's interesting. What kind of work? And why did he call you?'

'He's planning to demarcate some of the tribal territory for setting up a cooperative with their produce. But this plan has run into trouble because the state government wants to sell this land to some private entrepreneurs who wish to set up a cosmetic factory and a mall there. Now he's heard from a friend of Amritha's that Ashutosh Jethu has Left sympathies and fights for such injustice free of charge. He wants me to put in a word with Jethu. What do you think?'

'I think it's a jolly good cause and you should. Have you discussed this with Amritha?'

'Of course, it was Amritha who called me up first and told me how authentic the case was. She said Murugan was a close friend of Tanya, who was a colleague and good friend of hers. In fact, Murugan has invited both you and me to visit the tribal villages around Coonoor once before we speak to Ashutosh Jethu. What do you think?'

'That's not a bad idea. Maybe we could meet Murugan and learn something about the cooperative movement that he is organizing. It could be something worth trying out here, too.'

A week later...

Jhuma tried endlessly to contact Kishore on his mobile. The phone rang on and on till it got disconnected. After a quarter of an hour when Jhuma tried again, the recorded voice said that the mobile was switched off.

Jhuma was waiting for Kishore at the culvert near the marsh. He was supposed to be back from Purulia where he had gone for his personal investigations regarding the molestation of the Santhal girls. No one but Jhuma knew about it. The Purulia Express was due to return that morning at twelve noon. It was four p.m. and there was no message from Kishore as yet. Jhuma wondered: could Kishore have extended his visit by a day? But he would have surely rung up Jhuma to inform her. How callous of him not to bother, thought Jhuma as she turned back home.

When Jhuma went home, Ma was in the kitchen preparing the evening tea. She looked at Jhuma's face and exclaimed, 'What happened, Jhuma? You're looking pale. Are you not well?'

'No, I'm okay, just a bit tired.'

'Okay, wash your face and hands. Then have some luchi-alurdom that I've prepared for evening snacks.'

As Jhuma entered the bedroom, Bordi came and handed her some large envelopes that had come by post. A month back Jhuma had applied to IGNOU at Kishore's insistence, for doing their MA correspondence course. Jhuma had left off her studies after her BA Hons from City College to become a full-time member of the Party.

Suddenly, the land phone rang and Bordi picked up the receiver. She then passed on the receiver to Jhuma saying, 'It's for you.'

When Jhuma took the receiver, a male voice at the other end identified himself as Kishore's uncle. He said, 'Jhuma, there is terrible news for us. Kishore has had a fatal accident at the Howrah Station at one p.m. in the afternoon when he arrived by the Purulia Express. He was taken to NRS Hospital where he expired one hour back.

'Nooooooo,' shouted Jhuma, 'that's not true. Kishore-da can't be dead. You're lying, you're lying, you're lying.'

'Calm yourself, Jhuma, Kishore's old mother is out of her senses with grief. His body will be brought to his house tomorrow after post mortem and we will cremate him only in the evening. However, the senior Party leaders are all in the hospital. They are equally shocked by the news. Benoy Kanti is attending a meeting in Delhi. But he has sent his condolences from there. They are also trying hard to ensure that the post mortem is done promptly so that we don't have much hassle in getting the body released soon.'

After Kishore's uncle had called off, Jhuma went to her room, closed the door and burst into tears. There she lay in darkness the whole night weeping and moaning piteously.

***

When the first light of morning dawned, she sat up in bed remembering the last conversation that she had with Kishore. 'Kishore-da, they have killed you, they have killed you, they have killed you. And now they offer their hateful condolences, after wiping their slates clean. But I vow today to fulfil the dream that you had dreamt of building a cooperative farming system with Murugan among the tribals. Yes, Kishore-da, it will be hard, the path will be very lonely and difficult. Right from my teens whenever I was hurt or angry with the injustice of the world, you were there to counsel me and stand by me, steady as a rock. O Kishore-da, why, why are they so cruel? Why did they take you away from me—you were the only person who ever understood me. Life without you seems unliveable, the years stretching out from this morning like a desert endless. But Kishore-da, I'll live from today to fulfil only one dream and purpose, yours!

Angela 9

Dear Diary,

Today is the 24th of September, 2010. I have been inducted officially as the head of the brand new IDAC (Institute for the Differently Abled Child) Centre in Chennai. I don't know how to describe my feelings. I was feeling heady with a sense of power as I occupied the chair in my new room. Yet at the same time, I felt deeply humbled by the responsibility of my job. It makes me wonder how far I have travelled mentally and grown as a person in the last two years or so. Around two years from this day, my life had turned chaotic to say the least. Baby was born; Marc deserted me and I went to IDAC for help. Mrs Khastagir saw me through this very difficult period and did for me more than any parent could. Today, I can boast of the two closest friends I have in this wide world—Mrs Khastagir and Tanya.

Jhuma and Angela

When Jhuma got off the train at Coimbatore station with her backpack on her shoulders, a young boy of sixteen or so years, with a curly mop of hair, was waiting for them. He held a placard which read 'JHUMA *DIDI*'. Jhuma felt a strange sense of comfort at being called '*Didi*' by a virtual stranger and immediately her heart warmed towards her new relative. As she came forward to identify herself, he flashed a smile at her, showing his set of white teeth which gleamed against the ebony black of his skin. Then he took her luggage and indicated that they should move towards the exit.

'We take auto and go to bus stop,' he said in broken English.

Once they had got into the auto, Jhuma asked the boy, 'What is your name?'

'Dominic,' he replied, 'Murugan waiting for you in Coonoor—we take four hours to reach by bus.'

The bus stop was teeming with people but Dominic managed to get two tickets.

While Dominic slept, Jhuma looked out of the window, absorbing the new sights and sounds. After a long time, Jhuma felt her spirits lift. For a good four hours they travelled up the mountain slopes till they reached a market place. Dominic told Jhuma, 'We get down next stop.'

When the bus came to a halt, the conductor yelled, 'Coonoor, Coonoor.' They got down with two or three other people: an old woman with white hair with no slippers on her feet, an old bent man, and a young woman wearing a multi-coloured sari, a large nose ring, bangles made of shell, large-sized anklets and toe-rings on her feet. She was accompanied by two children, a girl of five or so years and a boy of three.

Jhuma decided to walk rather than take an auto-rickshaw. It was a mile's walk, said Dominic. Murugan was waiting for them in the parlour of the YWCA. He rose up to greet Jhuma and enquired about her journey. He said that she should have her meals and rest well. They would set out for Kotagiri the next morning. Dominic and Murugan were staying in the nearby YMCA.

Next day, prompt to his word, Murugan honked on the wheel of his jeep sharp at nine in the morning. Beside him sat Angela who had agreed to make a two-day trip to the Nilgiris, from the IDAC Centre in Chennai where she was presently working, to make a survey of the tribal villages.

Jhuma came out wearing a pair of jeans with a loose khadi top and sneakers on her feet. On her shoulder hung a jute bag. Her thick dark hair was tied into a single tight plait at the back. There was no trace of make-up on her face.

Murugan came out and introduced Angela to Jhuma. Jhuma smiled and told Angela that she had heard about her reason for coming to Coonoor. Angela's heart warmed towards the young girl.

After about an hour, Murugan said that they were approaching Kotagiri. From far they could see a cluster of huts. Murugan informed them that two civil servants of the then Madras Government, J.C. Whish and N.W. Kindersley, had made a journey to the hills in 1819. They went through a pass in the hills (now the village of Kil Kotagiri), and as reported back to their superiors, had 'discovered a tableland possessing a European climate'. They called the tableland 'Kotercherry'. Soon after, the Collector of Coimbatore, John Sullivan, journeyed into the hills and built himself a home in Kotagiri. He was the first European resident of the Nilgiri hills.

Once they reached the village, Murugan introduced Jhuma and Angela to the village headman. Murugan explained to them in their dialect that they had come to look after the women and children of the village.

The headman gave them an emblem of their clan painted on a stone as gifts. He explained to them that the Kota name is derived from 'Ko' which means king. The Kota people believe that their forefathers were kings. A place they live in is called a 'Kokkal'. The name 'Kota-giri' means 'mountain of the Kotas'. This was the meaning given by the Britishers. The Kota people were also called 'Kove', which means king.

Then they went on a tour of the village. Jhuma said that she had heard of the tradition that the faces of Kota boys were painted with blue paint. The headman explained that the Kotas painted their faces a ghost-like blue colour to signify the transformation of a boy to manhood at age nine-ten. 'We believe that in order to become a man, the child must die. The ghost-like blue paint is a reference to the death of childhood.'

Jhuma and Angela were overjoyed at the sight of some of the beautiful clay pottery that Murugan showed them. Murugan explained that the Kotas were traditional artisans and experts in the art of pottery and terracotta baking. And he wished to use this skill of theirs and market the wares produced by them for a fair price.

'But remember,' he warned the visitors, 'the biggest challenge is to win their trust and cooperation. The Kota tribe is known for their reclusiveness and their reluctance to meet or mix with any outsider. It's only because I'm here and since Simon the village headman has known me since childhood that he's allowed me to bring you here. Even then you would have noticed that none of the women and men have ventured out to come and meet us. You'll know the difference when you visit the Todas or the Kurumbas, they are far more open and approachable.'

From there, they travelled up the mountain road to the village of Tantiagiri. Here, Murugan took them to the village hospital built by Murugan. Dominic served them tea while they looked around the place. The hospital was housed in a thatched hut. But it was spotlessly clean and had quite a few modern facilities. The clinic was located at the entrance in a sunlit oblong shaped room with a row of windows opening out in the field. Four specialised doctors and a general physician sat in row behind partitioned screens. A large number of patients sat on the benches waiting for their turn. Some children accompanied by the adults played in the field outside.

Beside the clinic, there were three other huts which served as a hospital. Nurses were stationed in every hut to look after the hospitalised patients. A fourth hut served as a diagnostic laboratory with an X-ray and ECG machine and other such facilities.

'This hospital has been one of the high points of our

achievement to bring the good things of our modern civilization to this remote area. Even three years back, there was no doctor within a thirty-kilometre radius. The Kotas of course have their own highly developed knowledge of medicinal plants, but they need to compound it with modern allopathic treatment to get the best results. Not only this village but three other villages in this area can now boast of a mini hospital with a doctor on call 24/7.'

Here, Murugan paused for a while and said with a smile, 'That's more than probably what your developed district capitals in West Bengal can boast of.'

'Yes, the districts of West Bengal are woefully inadequate in terms of their medical infrastructure. So, the entire burden falls on the few government hospitals in Kolkata,' agreed Jhuma.

It was almost twilight by the time they finished their tour for the day. Murugan then told Jhuma and Angela, 'There's a little pucca building nearby, which we call *the hostel*. I've arranged for your stay there. Aunt Jurma will look after you there. She'll take good care of you even though the language barrier might prove a challenge. But I'm sure you'll manage. I'll come and take you around the village tomorrow.'

'Thank you,' said Jhuma and went along with Aunt Jurma. Inside the hostel, they were given two large rooms to stay in. Beds neatly draped with white bedsheets had been prepared on the floor. After Jhuma and Angela had freshened up, Aunt Jurma took them to a long, covered veranda with a row of benches and tables. Food was served on banana leaf. It was dried fish curry with dal and rice. Jhuma went to bed, feeling weary with the burden of carrying her hidden grief. Dusk had fallen and from the window she could see the crescent moon... 'Kishore-da, I have come to fulfil your dream, our dream...'

The next day the four again met for a tour of the Toda villages. Jhuma, who had been studying the Nilgiri tribes, began to ask Murugan questions about their survival.

'Is it true, Murugan, that the Todas are diminishing in number rapidly?'

'Yes, they are. Since the advent of the British, their cattle pastures have been slowly taken over and much of their land was converted into plantations, forcing them to abandon their traditional livelihood patterns. The Todas were by and large a pastoral people whose religion centred around the buffalo. So, dairy products were their chief trading products with the neighbouring Nilgiri people like the Badagas, the Kotas and the Kurumbas. With their pastoral lands shrinking, they are being forced out of their ethnic way of living. They often have to take jobs as labourers in plantations or as tailors, gardeners, etc., in Ooty. Our efforts as an NGO would be to save their ethnic way of life for them and that is why I am fighting a case for their rights instead of letting the corporates build malls and cosmetic factories here.'

As they toured the village, they came upon the *mund* of beehive houses which was the Toda home. Angela and Jhuma were much taken in by the sight of these barrel-shaped houses built of bamboos closely laid together, fastened with rattan and covered with thatch. They had small entrances and one had to get down on all fours to crawl in. But the most spectacular aspect of the village was the central temple which was conical in shape, and isolated from the rest of the village, with carvings of the sun, moon, buffaloes and other sacred icons.

Many Toda men, women and children took them around and showed them around the village while Murugan interpreted their language for Angela and Jhuma. They also discussed the exalted status of the dairy priest, and the elaborate rituals centred around the cult of the buffalo for which the priest had to maintain an extremely pristine way of life.

Angela pointed out that earlier, the Toda tribes followed fraternal polyandry where a woman married several brothers of the same family, but this practice had been discontinued. And they no longer wished to discuss such matters as they had been made to feel a sense of shame with the onslaught of modern civilization.

On their way back they discussed the effects of generations of inbreeding within the tribe caused by the self-imposed isolation of the tribe. Thus, congenital disease and sickness often got passed on from generation to generation. Angela remembered Tanya's words that she would have a cause to contribute to and realised that there was a lifetime of work waiting to be done. If she could help some helpless mothers struggling with their spastic children and give them a better life, her job would be well begun and from there they could take on so much more. If only Tanya, she and Jhuma could all work together, it would make a lot of difference! She had taken a great liking to this dedicated youngster. She began recounting her friendship with Tanya to Jhuma...

Murugan and Jhuma also discussed the economics of marketing the tribal farm produce in the urban market. There was an ever-increasing demand for 'organic' bio-friendly food products.

After they reached the hostel, the three of them, along with

Dominic, had their lunch together with Aunt Jurma. Afterwards, Murugan described his daily battles with the establishment. In turn, Jhuma shared her story of the dismal state of the peasants and the daily wage-earners in her own state. Sometimes, her voice would quaver with tears. Angela and Murugan listened to her respectfully, giving time to her to recover whenever she paused in mid-sentence. Before Murugan left, Jhuma called up her lawyer uncle Ashutosh Sengupta, who fought cases free of cost for various humanitarian issues. She told him all that she had learnt about Murugan's work for the tribals. Then Mr Sengupta spoke to Murugan and told him to make a trip to Delhi to discuss matters in detail. He also asked Murugan to bring him the documents for the case. They all felt jubilant after the call. Finally, Murugan decided to take his leave. He had to take an old woman to the hospital for treatment that night. Angela and Jhuma continued talking late up to the night.

Tanya 9

Six months later...

Tanya sat on the computer in her apartment checking her email. There was one from Angela in which she had sent some of Sonia's latest photographs taken on her birthday celebrated at the IDAC Centre in Chennai. It was almost five years since they had left New York. Tanya remembered her last conversation with Angela when the latter had asked her to leave her job here and join the movement for tribal children at Coonoor. She had refused that day promising Angela that she would join Murugan someday. Now perhaps was the time to redeem her pledge.

It had been three months since Murugan had been diagnosed with throat cancer. A week back he had been admitted in AIIMS in Delhi. When the news first reached Tanya, she felt gripped by a terrifying sense of agony. It gripped her whole being and left her paralysed with a sense of hopelessness about the future. Her whole being woke up to the full extent of her love for Murugan. She had removed herself from him, resisted his pleas to stay back and destroyed herself in the process of denying her love for him.

She had deliberately placed a vast geographical barrier between herself and him. Why did she do so? Wrecking his life as well as hers! Had they been together, this may not have happened; or even if it happened, they would have some happy memories and a common vision to live by. Now, while she had lost the past, the future she had temptingly promised herself had slipped away from her grasp. All that was left for her was a gaping sense of hopelessness.

After weeks of living in a paralytic state of agony, Tanya woke up from her torpor with a new sense of mission. She would go to Delhi to see Murugan and then settle permanently in the Nilgiris. She would carry on the work undertaken by Murugan as she envisioned herself ultimately doing. But the difference was that Murugan would not be beside her. She would be alone!

Angela called up that evening. 'Tanya, have you decided where you will stay when you come to the Nilgiris? Should I ask an agent to look up a good-sized furnished apartment for you in Coonoor? Or will you be sending some of that lovely furniture that you own down to Coonoor?'

'But Murugun stays in Kotagiri, doesn't he? I'm coming to work in his place, so I ought to stay in the same place.'

'Yes, he does. But he manages to live in a small shed above the medical centre. He owns very little furniture, just a cot, a chair and a table.'

'That's all I require, too. Could your agent get me a room like that close to Muru's? I'm going to dispose all my things before I leave. Half of my house is already empty and the rest will be packed and sent away before I leave.'

'When are you coming to India?'

'On the 19th of August. I am going to stay in Delhi for some time. From Delhi I will fly to Chennai, meet you and Sonia and then make my way up to the Nilgiris via Coimbatore.'

'What about your parents? Aren't you going to meet them in Kolkata?'

'Not now, maybe later. I spoke to Murugan. His fourth dose of chemotherapy is over. He's feeling a bit better. They will do a scan after two weeks to see if there's been any improvement. By then I will be there. Then they will continue the next phase. Angela, I wanted to tell you something. Murugan and I have decided to get married once I reach Delhi. This is the only way I could demonstrate what he means to me and to make up for not paying heed to his call when he had told me to stay on and work with him.'

'Tanya, that's wonderful. Can I come to Delhi with Sonia to celebrate the event with you?'

'That'll be great. I'd love to have you and Sonia with me on this important day of my life. You know that my family won't support me on this. They have never been able to reconcile themselves with my departure from the conventions of a traditional marriage. And... Angela, I spoke to Dr Reddy, his oncologist, on the phone today. He hasn't given me much to hope for... he says to be prepared for anything between six months to six years at the best.'

'How brave you are, Tanya!'

'Not brave, Angela. Murugan is my destiny; I can't fight it any longer. I have to be with him in his last days and then continue the unfinished work. We started it together.'

Epilogue

Three months later...
    As the plane touched ground in Coimbatore, Tanya walked to the exit gate with her small suitcase. It consisted of all the possessions she had in the world.
    As she adjusted her eyes to the bright morning light, four figures emerged from the shadows. Treading lightly with arms stretched, a little petite figure with a head of dark curls rushed towards her, hugging her: 'Aunt Tanya, how I missed you.' Tanya looked up at the child in wonder: 'Baby Mamma! My Baby Mamma!'
    On the heels of her seven-year-old daughter came the mother, with a smile of comfort as she remembered from long ago, like the reels of an old film come to life again.

Time and distance vanished as the friends embraced each other. Suddenly, Angela swung right and brought into their common embrace a shy young girl. 'And here, dear Tanya, is Jhuma of whom you've heard so much.'
    Holding Jhuma and Angela's hands in her own, with Baby Mamma in her own, Tanya felt a new stirring in her anguished heart.
    'It is right we are all here together,' she said calmly, 'and there is much to do. We belong no longer to our past; it is to our present that we must look. There are many who need us. To them, we give our future.'